ENCYCLOPEDIA of BIRDS

WIDE EYED EDITIONS

CONTENTS

4–5	INTRODUCTION FROM THE AUTHOR	28–33	GROUNDBIRDS
6–7	WHAT IS A BIRD?	34–39	HOLE-NESTERS
8–9	A GUIDE TO BIRD FAMILIES	40–43	LANDFOWL
		44–47	OWLS
10–15	BIRDS OF TORPOR	48–55	PARROTS AND ALLIES
16–27	BIRDS OF PREY	56–139	PERCHING BIRDS

140–141   **PIGEONS AND DOVES**

142–145   **TUNNEL-NESTERS**

146–177   **WATERBIRDS**

178–185   **FORGOTTEN BIRDS**

186–187   **GET TO KNOW BIRDS NEAR YOU**

188–189   **INDEX**

190–191   **GLOSSARY**

HOW TO USE THIS BOOK

CHAPTER HEADER: Learn about how the species on these pages are linked together.

LATIN NAME: Each species has a scientific Latin name that is the same in all languages.

NAVIGATION: Use these handy tabs to work out which group of animals you are reading about.

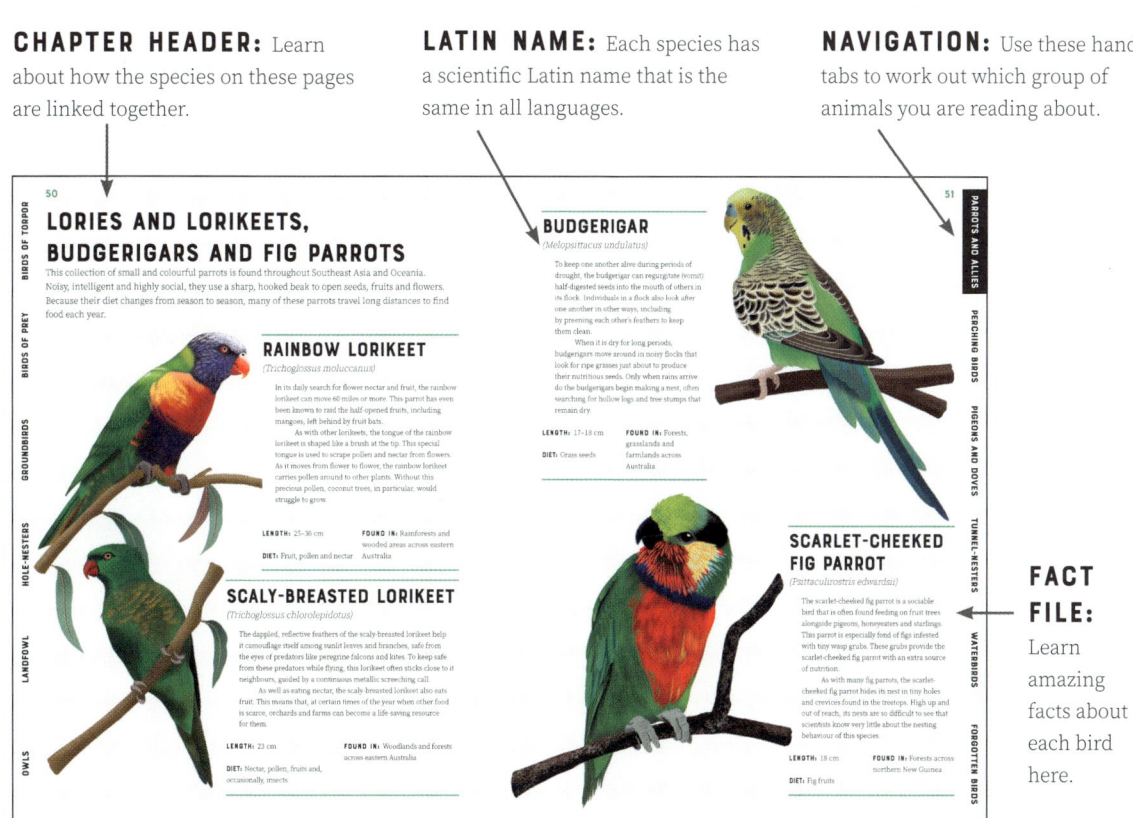

FACT FILE: Learn amazing facts about each bird here.

You can read this book in any order and in any number of sittings. Read it in your armchair, or take it out into the wild. Read about the birds you know you love, and then discover many more you had no idea existed!

INTRODUCTION FROM THE AUTHOR

OPEN YOUR WINDOW AND HAVE A LISTEN! IF YOU WAIT LONG ENOUGH, YOU ARE ALMOST CERTAIN TO HEAR A BIRD.

You may hear a short whistle or a piping alarm call. You may hear a pair of birds chirping to one another to keep in touch. You may, if you are lucky, hear the stirring tune of a songbird or the mewing of a bird of prey high in the sky. These birds live out their entire lives in our spaces. Or rather, we live out ours in theirs, for birds have been around a lot longer than we have. This was their world, long before it was ours...

Since the death of their dinosaur relatives sixty-six million years ago, birds have done rather well for themselves. Today, more than 10,000 species are known from all over the world. Birds live in almost every habitat on Earth, from the coldest, snowiest slopes to the warmest, driest deserts.

Birds dive in our seas and soar in our skies. There are birds that can swim, birds that can skate across water, birds that can run, and birds that can glide for hours, barely flapping their wings. There are some, like swifts, that can spend more than a year in the air before coming back down to Earth. These, truly, are animals that need to be seen to be believed. And that's where this book comes in...

This encyclopedia of birds contains more than 300 bird species, carefully chosen to show the dizzying diversity of birds that exist out there in the world. These birds have been brought to life through wonderful painted illustrations by Namasri Niumim, whose artworks show spectacular animals that are often colorful, often dynamic, and always charismatic.

While putting this book together, we had one thing on our minds. It was to awaken you, the reader, to the extraordinary beauty of birds all over the world. We wanted to grow your interest in all the different families of birds that are out there, each with their own incredible behaviors, eye-catching fashions, and curious habits. And, importantly, we also wanted to include some of the things we have yet to learn about birds along the way, including mysterious birds who live in remote places that scientists struggle to reach or birds that are on the very edge of extinction, disappearing for reasons known and unknown.

We hope that after you read this book, you start to notice the birds in your everyday life, on your way to school or walking to the shops: the sparrows gathering on the rooftops, the wrens dashing through leaves, the swallows twisting and turning above, the soft cooing of a backyard pigeon in spring. If you notice any of these things after reading this book, we'll be very proud.

So, enjoy this book, take it all in, and as you revisit its pages again and again, keep your windows open, so that birds continue to be a very real part of your life.

You really do live in a world of birds. It's up to us, as animal-lovers and scientists, young and old, to keep it that way for as long as possible.

WHAT IS A BIRD?

Birds are the only surviving branch of the dinosaur family tree. For this reason, today's birds share many features that dinosaurs, particularly the group that includes the *Tyrannosaurus rex*, once had.

FEATHERS

For many dinosaurs, feathers were only used for insulation and decoration, but for birds, some feathers have been modified for flight. Feathers come in two types: rigid or downy. Rigid feathers are streamlined, strong and smooth, helping birds stay airborne. Downy feathers are softer and shorter, helping with insulation.

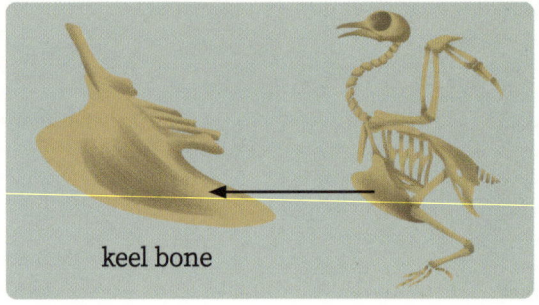

keel bone

BONES

Birds have hollow bones to reduce their overall weight. This helps them stay in the air for longer. Birds also have a very large bone in the chest, known as the keel bone, where the wing muscles attach. The keel acts like an anchor to support flight muscles, especially during lift-off.

WINGS

Much of a bird's wing is held in shape by long finger bones, most notably the alula, which is the equivalent of a dinosaur's thumb. When flexing this bone, birds can spread their wings extra wide, which is important when slowing down or landing. Inside the wing, birds have lots of muscles that allow the bones and feathers to flex in many ways—this is what makes birds so agile in the air.

rigid

downy

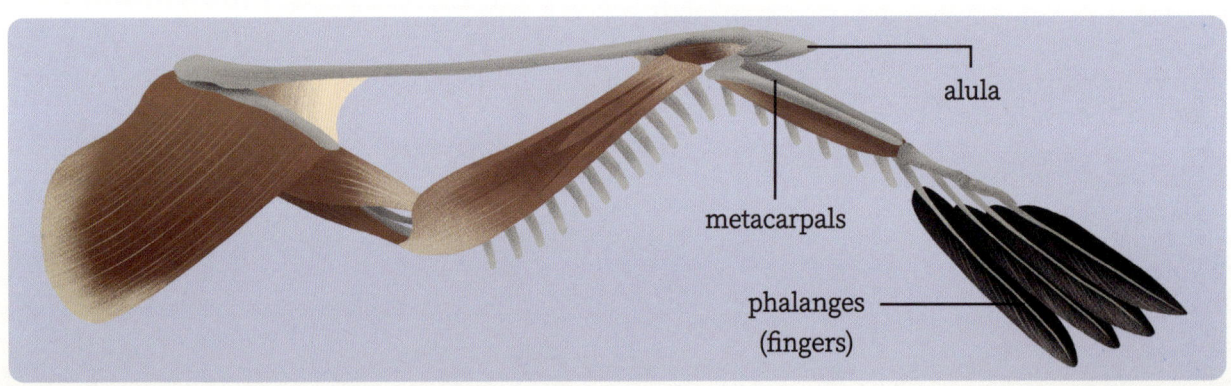

alula

metacarpals

phalanges (fingers)

NESTS

Like many dinosaurs did, birds lay eggs with hard shells. Nearly all birds make nests out of material gathered from their environment. Some build bowl-shaped or sphere-shaped nests, while others dig burrows, which they line with grasses or feathers. Because of the threat of predators raiding their nests, male and female birds often work together to raise their young. In some species, birds form loyal pairs that stay together for years.

BEAKS

Unlike dinosaurs, which mostly had teeth, birds have a beak covered in special armor known as keratin. Each bird has a beak suited to the foods that it eats. Fish-eating birds often have a long beak that they can stab into the water like a harpoon. Vultures have a hooked beak for tearing apart dead animals, and finches have stout, short beaks adapted for pulling apart seeds.

fish-eating heron

vulture

finch

A GUIDE TO BIRD FAMILIES

Scientists have discovered more than 10,000 different kinds of birds, and the number is still rising. Sometimes, this is because scientists discover new types of birds from far-away jungles or hard-to-reach volcanic islands. Other times, scientists look at an existing species and realize that it is actually two different species that look very alike.

Special scientists known as taxonomists have the tricky job of trying to work out where to place newly discovered birds in the bird family tree. To help them do this, many scientists look at molecular codes that animals carry within their cells, known as DNA. Closely related animals have very similar DNA, which makes the job of grouping birds into a family tree a little bit easier.

Most birds on Earth are from a single family group, known as passerines, or often simply called "perching birds." These birds have three forward-pointing toes and one toe that points backward on each foot, meaning they can grip objects in their environment, especially twigs and branches while resting.

Other large bird groups include owls, ducks, and parrots. There are many bird groups that contain only a handful of species. These include the snake-eating seriemas of South America and the colorful cuckoo-rollers of Africa. In this book, we have placed the smallest groups into "Forgotten Birds." This is because their groups are so tiny they are often mistakenly grouped with other birds.

MATING MADNESS

To make things even more tricky, males and females of many bird species look very different. In many birds, males look more colorful or showy than females. This is because they have evolved shiny or colorful feathers as a way to advertise to females how healthy they are, and what excellent parents they might make if given the chance.

NIGHTJARS, FROGMOUTHS, AND OILBIRDS

With small feet and long pointed wings, these unusual birds were once placed together in a single group, the Caprimulgidae, a name that means "goat-suckers." They got this name because centuries ago people believed these secretive birds stole milk from goats at night. Like others in their group, these birds can enter a sleepy state known as "torpor," which saves them energy

COMMON PAURAQUE
(Nyctidromus albicollis)

The common pauraque hides in forests during the day before emerging to hunt moths across rivers and grasslands at night. Its scientific name, *Nyctidromus*, means "night-racer" in Ancient Greek.

Like other nightjars, the pauraque incubates its eggs on the floor without making a nest. It depends heavily on its camouflage to protect itself from predators, including cats and dogs. Having longer legs than other nightjars, this species often runs away from predators on the ground, rather than take to the wing.

LENGTH: 28–30 cm

DIET: Flying insects

FOUND IN: Forest edges and grasslands across South America, Central America, and parts of the USA

EURASIAN NIGHTJAR
(Caprimulgus europaeus)

From its perch, the Eurasian nightjar scans the evening sky, looking for prey. Its large eyes contain a special reflective layer that allows it to spot the passing silhouettes of moths and other nocturnal insects. Long, whisker-like hairs on the beak help the nightjar "feel" for prey as it gets within striking distance of the beak.

Being camouflaged, these ground-nesting birds are hard to spot. Their location is most often given away by their loud, grasshopper-like song, which can be heard from half a kilometer away.

LENGTH: 24–28 cm

DIET: Large insects, including moths, beetles, dragonflies, and cockroaches

FOUND IN: Breeds in grasslands and heathlands across Europe and Asia and tundra in remote North America

TAWNY FROGMOUTH
(Podargus strigoides)

During the day, the tawny frogmouth is one of the most camouflaged of all birds. Its feather patterns mimic the dried-up branches of fallen trees, meaning that when it rests in these places, it seems to disappear. Staying statue-still is important to the display. Adults regularly use a special call that instructs their young to freeze in position should a predator approach.

To stop itself from overheating while resting in this position, the tawny frogmouth produces special mucus that cools incoming air before it reaches the lungs. If the heat continues to rise, the frogmouth begins to pant, like a dog.

LENGTH: 34–53 cm

DIET: Large insects, millipedes, centipedes, and spiders

FOUND IN: Forests and scrublands across Australia and central USA

OILBIRD
(Steatornis caripensis)

The oilbird is the world's only nocturnal fruit-eating bird. Like a bat, it navigates in the dark by listening to how its "click-click" calls reflect off nearby objects. This is called echolocation. Like bats, the oilbird also nests in cave colonies, sometimes numbering 15,000 individuals or more.

Oilbird nests are made from droppings and regurgitated (vomited) fruits, mixed up to make a cement-like paste. Within the nest, up to four eggs are sat upon frequently to keep them from getting too cold in the cool interior of the cave.

LENGTH: 41–49 cm

DIET: Fruits

FOUND IN: Remote forests beside rocky caves and canyons

SWIFTS, SWIFTLETS, AND TREESWIFTS

These agile, insect-hunting birds look like swallows, but they are more closely related to hummingbirds. Their speed is partly down to their unique wing bones, which rotate more flexibly at their base. This allows them to generate speed on both the upstroke and the downstroke of each flap of the wings. They use such a huge amount of energy that sometimes they need to take a hibernation-like rest, known as torpor.

COMMON SWIFT
(Apus apus)

The common swift can spend almost a full year in the sky, only coming down to nest and rear chicks. This means that, moving seasonally north and south each year, a single swift can clock up more than two million miles in its lifetime, equivalent to flying to the Moon and back four times over. No other bird in the world spends so much of its life airborne.

This dynamic insect-hunter regularly flies at speeds of 60 miles per hour or more. Often, when insects swarm over wetlands, many swifts come together in great flocks that number more than 1,000 individuals. While flying, swifts shriek loudly to one another, forming what birdwatchers call a "screaming party."

Like hummingbirds, swifts can enter a deep sleep known as torpor, which slows down their heart rate and metabolism. Swift hatchlings depend on this adaptation to save energy while their parents are out hunting. Swifts build their nests out of materials that they catch in the sky, held together with special gloopy saliva.

LENGTH: 16–18 cm

DIET: Insects

FOUND IN: Breeds in insect-rich habitats across northern Africa, Europe and Asia

HIMALAYAN SWIFTLET
(Aerodramus brevirostris)

Like a bat, the Himalayan swiftlet can navigate caves using sound. It does this by sending special clicks into the air and listening to how these sounds reflect off the walls of the cave. Among birds, this adaptation (known as echolocation) is known only in swiftlets and oilbirds.

The tiny cup-nest of the Himalayan swift, made from the bird's saliva, is glued to the wall of a cave, often within touching distance of other swiftlet nests. Each of their shiny white eggs is barely the size of a grape.

LENGTH: 13–14 cm

DIET: Insects

FOUND IN: Especially common in river valleys of the Himalayas

CRESTED TREESWIFT
(Hemiprocne coronata)

As the name suggests, the crested treeswift makes its nest in trees. It uses saliva to glue a cup-shaped construction, made of feathers and bark, to the sunniest sides of branches. From a distance, this camouflaged nest looks like a natural bump or knobble in the bark of the tree.

Should a predator, such as a hungry bird or lizard, approach the nest, crested treeswift hatchlings appear to freeze, often with their beaks held slightly upward. This helps them blend in with nearby twigs and branches.

LENGTH: 23–25 cm

DIET: Insects

FOUND IN: Open forests and woodlands throughout South and Southeast Asia

HUMMINGBIRDS

Hummingbirds use their long beaks to drink nectar while hovering in front of flowers. They might look motionless, but their wings are actually beating so fast that they produce a humming sound, hence the name. More than 350 species of these uniquely active birds are known, mostly from South America. Hummingbird torpor can last a few hours or a whole night.

BEE HUMMINGBIRD
(Mellisuga helenae)

Barely the size of an adult human's thumb, the bee hummingbird is the smallest bird in the world. Its size helps it to retrieve nectar from smaller flowers that larger hummingbirds cannot reach with their broader beaks. It weighs approximately the same as a paper clip.

Bee hummingbirds court one another using the sound of their tail feathers as a display. As they hover, these feathers flutter and vibrate. Its cup-shape nest, made of tiny scraps of bark held together with spider silk, is big enough to hold just two eggs, each the size of a raisin.

Moving at speeds of thirty miles an hour, the bee hummingbird can visit 1,500 flowers in a single day. It hovers by rapidly flapping its wings, sometimes at a rate of more than 200 times a second. For their size, hummingbirds burn oxygen ten times faster than a human athlete, which means they require lots of energy. To stay alive, some hummingbirds need to swallow half their body weight in sugar-rich nectar each day.

LENGTH: 5–6 cm

DIET: Nectar and small insects

FOUND IN: Woodlands and swamplands of Cuba and surrounding islands

GIANT HUMMINGBIRD
(Patagona gigas)

The giant hummingbird weighs ten times more than the bee hummingbird, meaning its wings have to work extra-hard to stay airborne. During peak activity, the giant hummingbird's heart beats more than 1,000 times each minute to keep its muscles supplied with fresh oxygen.

As with other hummingbirds, the giant hummingbird enters a deeper state of sleep than other birds. This is known as torpor. By lowering its heart rate and slowing the rate at which it absorbs food, torpor allows hummingbirds to save energy at night.

LENGTH: 23 cm

DIET: Nectar and small insects

FOUND IN: Shrubby hillsides throughout the Andes mountain range in South America

RUBY-THROATED HUMMINGBIRD
(Archilochus colubris)

Every spring, the ruby-throated hummingbird journeys from South America to North America, often flying for more than 500 miles without stopping for food or water. This epic journey is powered by fat reserves stored in the weeks before travel.

As it moves between continents, the ruby-throated hummingbird remains watchful for its main predator, hummingbird-hunting hawks. But, being small, hummingbirds can fall prey to other predators too, including dragonflies and even, should they become entangled in a web, spiders.

LENGTH: 7.5–9 cm

DIET: Nectar

FOUND IN: South and North American forests, orchards, and gardens, seasonally

EAGLES AND OSPREYS

With sharp eyes and hooked beaks, these fearsome birds can be found all over the world. They are part of a larger group of birds of prey that includes hawks, vultures, and kites. This group is known as the Accipitriformes, from the Latin *accipiter*, meaning "hawk."

BALD EAGLE
(Haliaeetus leucocephalus)

The bald eagle builds the biggest tree nest in the animal kingdom. Some nests can be bigger than a car! At 5.6 kilograms, the bald eagle is one of the heaviest eagles, and needs a large nest that can support its weight.

The bald eagle does not have a bald head as the name suggests. Instead, its name comes from the old meaning of the word bald, "white-headed." The long, hooked yellow beak is used for stripping chunks of meat from its fish prey.

WINGSPAN: 168–244 cm

DIET: Fish

FOUND IN: Wetlands, marshlands, and coastal regions across North America

PHILIPPINE EAGLE
(Pithecophaga jefferyi)

Unlike other birds of prey, this secretive predator often hunts in pairs. While one eagle captures the attention of its prey, the other swoops in unseen from behind. Once thought to eat only monkeys, scientists now realize that this eagle has an appetite for many animals, including small deer and even other birds of prey.

The Philippine eagle is the national bird of the Philippines. The killing of this bird of prey is strictly against the law and can result in up to twelve years in jail.

WINGSPAN: 184–202 cm

DIET: Many animals, including small deer, rats, monkeys, and reptiles, especially snakes

FOUND IN: Remote mountain forests across much of the Philippines

STELLER'S SEA EAGLE
(Haliaeetus pelagicus)

Upon broad wings more than 2 meters across, the Steller's sea eagle soars over shallow waters, scanning the surface for fish. When prey is spotted, it grasps its meal with powerful, hooked claws. Special patterns of bumps, called spicules, are found upon its toes. Spicules stop slippery fish from falling to safety as the eagle flies away.

Like many birds of prey, the Stellar's sea eagle makes a screeching call that travels for hundreds of meters. These calls are both a symbol of strength and a warning to rivals to keep well away.

WINGSPAN: 195–245 cm

DIET: Fish, including cod and salmon

FOUND IN: Coastal regions of northeastern Asia

OSPREY
(Pandion haliaetus)

When grappling with fish, the osprey can close its nostrils to keep out water. Its oily feathers are waterproof, meaning that the osprey can launch itself back into the sky straight after making its kill without needing to dry out.

Like many birds of prey, ospreys regularly migrate between wintering grounds and nesting grounds, returning to the same nest each year. Some osprey nests have been used annually for seventy years or more.

WINGSPAN: 150–180 cm

DIET: Fish

FOUND IN: Wetland habitats on every continent except Antarctica

FALCONS AND CARACARAS

Falcons are the most agile and dynamic of all birds of prey, with many species able to catch airborne animals, such as bats and other birds, mid-flight. They differ slightly from their close relatives, the caracaras, who prefer scavenging the remains of dead animals (carrion).

PEREGRINE FALCON
(Falco peregrinus)

There is no faster animal on Earth than the peregrine falcon. As it drops down on its prey from high above, it can reach speeds of 200 miles per hour—as fast as an arrow shot from a bow. This so-called stoop attack is so fast it can be impossible for other birds, such as pigeons and doves, to spot. The prey, stunned or instantly killed, is captured mid-air as it falls and is later eaten back at the nest.

The peregrine falcon has many special adaptations to fly at high speed. An extra pair of see-through eyelids perform the role of flight goggles, while bony bumps and bobbles in the falcon's nostrils stop air flooding into the lungs as it descends sharply. The characteristic mustache-like pattern below the eyes (called the malar stripe) helps reduce glare from the sun, allowing the falcon to see prey more clearly as it maneuvres in the sky.

WINGSPAN: 79–114 cm

DIET: Medium-sized birds, including pigeons and seabirds

FOUND IN: Mountain ranges, valleys, and cities, where it roosts on high buildings, worldwide

PYGMY FALCON
(Polihierax semitorquatus)

Weighing little more than a tennis ball, the pygmy falcon is one of the world's smallest birds of prey. Its lightweight body means it can use the abandoned nests of smaller birds, particularly weaver birds, whose nests keep especially cool during the hottest parts of the day.

Like all falcons, the pygmy falcon rarely kills with its claws. Instead, its killer blow comes from a scissor-like blade on the beak known as the tomial tooth.

WINGSPAN: 34–40 cm

DIET: Mostly insects and small reptiles, especially lizards

FOUND IN: Dry bushlands of southern and eastern Africa

BLACK CARACARA
(Daptrius ater)

The black caracara is a jack-of-all-trades. In a single day, it uses lots of different tricks to find food—from raiding bird nests and gleaning insects off leaves to scavenging leftovers from humans. This species is even known to land upon large mammals, such as tapirs, and peck at their blood-sucking ticks.

The black caracara also hunts fish, finding the narrow parts of rivers where migrating fish become squashed together, and attacking again and again with beak and talons.

WINGSPAN: 91–100 cm

DIET: Plants, seeds, animals, and carrion

FOUND IN: Subtropical and tropical forests across much of South America

PARROTS AND ALLIES | PERCHING BIRDS | PIGEONS AND DOVES | TUNNEL-NESTERS | WATERBIRDS | FORGOTTEN BIRDS

HAWKS

With large eyes and a hooked beak, hawks are dynamic predators. Some hawks are capable of hunting other birds while they fly, twisting and turning quickly to catch their prey. Along with eagles, kites, harriers, and most vultures, hawks are an important member of the bird-of-prey group known as the Accipitridae, one of three subgroups in the larger Accipitriformes group.

AFRICAN HARRIER HAWK
(Polyboroides typus)

The African harrier hawk glides low over the forest canopy, waiting eagerly for smaller birds to appear and aggressively chase it away. When this happens, it knows that a nest is nearby. Later, it will return to the nest to feed on the chicks.

Like other hawks, the African harrier hawk hunts either from a perch or while soaring high above and scanning the floor for movement. This aerial technique is especially useful for spotting lizards.

LENGTH: 51–68 cm

DIET: Birds, small lizards and snakes, and the fruit of the oil palm

FOUND IN: Rainforests, farmlands, and near some towns and cities, mostly in tropical regions of western Africa

HAWAIIAN HAWK
(Buteo solitarius)

Hunting from a perch, its eyes scanning for movement, the Hawaiian hawk makes an excellent ratcatcher. Its appetite for these animals is helpful, because rats frequently raid the nests of other Hawaiian birds, sometimes causing native species to become extinct. Rats have contributed to the extinction of more than thirty Hawaiian bird species in the last 250 years.

In Hawaiʻi, local people know this bird as *ʻio*. This is because this word sounds like its loud mating call, a rasping "eeeh-oh" that echoes through the forest.

LENGTH: 41–46 cm

DIET: Rats, lizards, large insects, and some birds

FOUND IN: Forests and farmlands of Hawaiʻi's Big Island

EURASIAN GOSHAWK
(Accipiter gentilis)

Bursting off its perch at speeds of almost 40 miles per hour, most goshawk attacks are over in seconds. The long tail is used to help dodge and weave through branches. Because the goshawk rarely flaps its wings, this bird of prey makes almost no sound during the chase. Its prey is often taken totally by surprise, squeezed to death by the muscular talons.

Like other hawks, the Eurasian goshawk takes its prey to special "plucking perches," where it removes the feathers from the carcass before swallowing it. It will often use the same perch again and again.

LENGTH: 55–61 cm

DIET: Squirrels, rabbits, hares, birds, and some reptiles

FOUND IN: Deciduous and coniferous forests throughout Europe and Asia

GALÁPAGOS HAWK
(Buteo galapagoensis)

The Galápagos hawk is far from picky. Insects, centipedes, lizards, rats, and snakes are just some of the animals it hunts. It even attacks marine iguanas that rival it for size and weight.

Unlike most hawks, the Galápagos hawk frequently hunts in packs. Soaring up to 200 meters in the air, two or three hawks search the ground, calling out when they see a potential meal. On the ground, the largest hawk is allowed to feed first, before the smaller hawks are invited forward to eat the rest.

LENGTH: 45–56 cm

DIET: Many animals found in the Galápagos Islands

FOUND IN: Scattered throughout the western islands of the Galápagos Islands

KITES

These birds of prey are closely related to hawks, eagles, and the vultures of Africa and Asia. Most kites have short beaks and long, narrow wings and tails. Kites in some parts of the world perform the same role as vultures, cleaning up dead animals through scavenging.

RED KITE
(Milvus milvus)

To survive, the red kite takes what it can. As well as consuming dead sheep and pigs, it regularly soars over busy roads, looking out for animals killed by cars and trucks. When times get especially hard, the red kite can survive off a diet of earthworms.

In many countries, including the UK and Ireland, the red kite almost became extinct in the last hundred years. This was mostly because humans killed red kites fearing that they could eat farm animals. Recent reintroductions have seen their numbers recover swiftly in these places.

WINGSPAN: 143–171 cm

DIET: Carrion, worms, small voles and mice, rabbits, and wounded birds

FOUND IN: Forests, woodlands, and farmlands throughout Europe

BLACK KITE
(Milvus migrans)

Numbering six million or more, the black kite is the most numerous bird of prey in the world. The success of this kite is mainly due to its talent for spotting new ways to find food. In cities, particularly in India, the black kite regularly eats garbage and other human waste.

In other parts of the world, the black kite is even more wily. It has been known to scan the edges of forest fires to catch prey fleeing the heat. There is even evidence that, by carrying burning twigs from place to place, the black kite can start fires elsewhere.

WINGSPAN: 120–153 cm

DIET: Animals, dead or alive, including mice, rats, and fish

FOUND IN: Various habitats throughout Europe, Africa, Asia, and Australasia

SNAIL KITE
(*Rostrhamus sociabilis*)

With the precision of a surgeon, the snail kite uses its hooked beak to carefully remove freshwater snails from their shells. It then carefully separates out the foul-tasting parts of the snail's slimy body and swallows the rest. Preparing its meal in this way can take less than a minute.

As with many birds of prey, the snail kite often uses the same perch to pull apart its kills after each hunt. Scientists find these perches by looking for tell-tale piles of empty snail shells, sometimes numbering 1,000 or more.

WINGSPAN: 99–120 cm

DIET: Snails

FOUND IN: Wetlands across South America, the Caribbean, and central and southern Florida, USA

MISSISSIPPI KITE
(*Ictinia mississippiensis*)

The Mississippi kite travels between North America and South America each year, clocking up thousands of miles. Mostly, it moves in small flocks of twenty to thirty birds but on occasion it forms super-flocks with other birds of prey, sometimes 10,000 or more in number.

In both North and South America, the Mississippi kite is often spotted near horses or cattle. When these large animals move, insects are flushed from nearby grasses, which the Mississippi kite catches and eats.

WINGSPAN: 75–83 cm

DIET: Insects, especially cicadas and grasshoppers

FOUND IN: Forests and farmlands across North and South America

AMERICAN VULTURES

Though they look similar, these large birds of prey are not closely related to the vultures that live in Africa, Europe, and Asia. While soaring, many of these vultures use their nostrils to detect the smell of dead animals (carrion) on the ground. Because these birds do not have a voice box, their calls are made of hissing and grunting sounds.

ANDEAN CONDOR
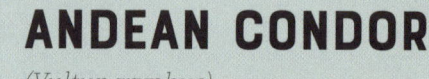
(Vultur gryphus)

The Andean condor is the largest bird of prey in the world. Its broad wings, each as long as a person, help it to glide for long periods without flapping. To generate more lift, saving valuable energy, the Andean condor rises on gusts of upward-moving air known as thermals, generated when rock faces are heated by the sun.

In a single day, the Andean condor can cruise for more than 120 miles. Mostly, this American vulture homes in on special chemical scents given off by decaying animals, including llamas, cattle, and even dead dolphins and whales washed onto shore. Occasionally, the Andean condor will also fly toward other circling vultures to see what they have found. Being so large, the Andean condor can easily bully smaller vultures away from a potential meal.

By removing dead animals from the environment, the Andean condor, like other condors and vultures, reduces the number of places where diseases can multiply. This, along with its majestic size and grace, has seen the Andean condor become a celebrated bird in many South American countries.

WINGSPAN: 260–320 cm

DIET: Carrion and, less commonly, birds and their eggs

FOUND IN: The Andes and Santa Marta mountain ranges in South America

KING VULTURE
(Sarcoramphus papa)

Smaller vultures often wait patiently for the king vulture to appear at a rotting carcass. This is because its hooked beak is the only thing powerful enough to tear through thick skin. The king vulture feeds first, using a long, sandpaper-like tongue to strip meat from bones. Only when its stomach is full does it let other vultures have their turn to feed.

Like many vultures and condors of South America, the king vulture has a bald, featherless head. This makes the face easier to clean after it has been plunged into the body of a dead animal.

WINGSPAN: 150 cm

DIET: Rotting animals

FOUND IN: Tropical forests and grasslands throughout South America

CALIFORNIA CONDOR
(Gymnogyps californianus)

Three decades ago, the California condor almost faced extinction. Its numbers fell very sharply because of accidental poisoning, hunting (poaching), and collisions with powerlines. Thankfully, right before their disappearance, scientists stepped in. By rearing condor chicks in captivity, new generations of wild condors were reared-up and released.

Currently, there are more than 250 California condors living wild, some reaching ages of 60 years, and more releases are planned. Thanks to the hard work of scientists, North America's largest bird is back from the brink.

WINGSPAN: 280 cm

DIET: Carrion, especially deer, goats, sheep, donkeys, and horses

FOUND IN: Shrublands and forests of California, USA

VULTURES

Found throughout many parts of Africa, Europe, and Asia, vultures are scavengers of dead animals. Most species have bald heads and hooked beaks for tearing apart their food. Though they resemble American vultures and condors, this group are more closely related to eagles, buzzards, kites, and hawks.

LAPPET-FACED VULTURE
(Torgos tracheliotos)

Smaller vultures avoid the lappet-faced vulture, the angriest and most aggressive of African vultures. Its powerful beak can tear through the toughest of animal skin and pull apart bones and tendons that other scavengers ignore.

In a single sitting, a lappet-faced vulture can eat a kilogram or more of meat, equivalent to the weight of a watermelon. This means that, after particularly big meals, some vultures can struggle to fly.

LENGTH: 120 cm

DIET: Mostly carrion

FOUND IN: Dry savannas and deserts throughout Africa and the Middle East

WHITE-RUMPED VULTURE
(Gyps bengalensis)

Upon seeing a carcass, the white-rumped vulture descends quickly and feeds as fast as it can, before more aggressive scavengers arrive. A pack of white-rumped vultures can clean up a dead cow in as little as twenty minutes.

Like many vultures, the white-rumped vulture is threatened with extinction. This is partly because vultures that feed on dead farm animals can be poisoned by human-made medicines used in farming. Forty years ago, there were millions of white-rumped vultures. Now, just 6,000 remain.

LENGTH: 76–93 cm

DIET: Carrion

FOUND IN: Open countrysides throughout South and Southeast Asia

BEARDED VULTURE
(Gypaetus barbatus)

The bearded vulture is the only bird in the world that can survive almost exclusively on a diet of bones. Inside its stomach, some of the most powerful acids in the animal kingdom help turn its meal into a nutritious gloop.

The sturdy beak of the bearded vulture can shatter bones as thick as a golf club. When bones are too large or tough, this vulture carries them to a height of up to 150 meters and drops them onto rocky ground, where they smash into smaller, more digestible chunks.

LENGTH: 94–125 cm

DIET: Mostly bones

FOUND IN: Scattered across mountain ranges and open plains in Africa, Europe, and Asia

RÜPPELL'S VULTURE
(Gyps rueppelli)

The Rüppell's vulture is the highest-flying bird in the world. It can soar to a height of more than 10 kilometers, which is more than 1,000 meters higher than Mount Everest. Like other vultures, it soars by locating upward-moving currents of air, often generated when the sun heats up rocky areas on the ground.

Soaring saves vultures energy and also gives a good vantage point from which to spot dead or dying animals on the ground. Unlike American vultures and condors, the Rüppell's vulture relies on sight, not smell, to find a potential meal.

LENGTH: 101 cm

DIET: Carrion

FOUND IN: Grasslands, mountains, and woodlands across sub-Saharan Africa

EMUS, KIWIS, AND CASSOWARIES

Distantly related to ostriches, the emus, kiwis, and cassowaries are completely flightless. Together, these birds are known as ratites. All ratites have an excellent sense of smell, which is used to find food. Many possess sharp claws that can be used for defence against predators that stalk them on the ground.

EMU
(Dromaius novaehollandiae)

Taller than many humans, the emu is second only to the ostrich in height. Its long, dashing strides, some more than 2 meters in length, help it to accelerate quickly. Emus regularly reach speeds of 30 miles per hour or more, mostly when running away from danger.

Millions of years ago, emus lived alongside a host of Australian predators that are now extinct. Prehistoric predators of emu included giant lizards and flesh-eating kangaroos.

HEIGHT: 150–190 cm

DIET: Leaves, seeds, fruits, and small animals, including grasshoppers, beetles, and cockroaches

FOUND IN: Woodlands, forests, and dry scrublands across many parts of Australia

NORTH ISLAND BROWN KIWI
(Apteryx mantelli)

Relative to its size, the North Island brown kiwi lays the largest eggs of all birds. Though this species is roughly the same size as a chicken, it lays eggs that are about six times larger. These giant eggs give kiwi chicks plenty of space to grow, so when they hatch they are ready to run away from predators almost straight away.

Kiwis are guided to food using a strong sense of smell, powered by a pair of nostrils at the end of the beak, rather than at the base of the beak like in other birds.

HEIGHT: 50–65 cm

DIET: Mostly insects and worms

FOUND IN: Forests throughout New Zealand's North Island

SOUTHERN CASSOWARY
(*Casuarius casuarius*)

The southern cassowary spends most of its day smelling for fallen fruits, especially fruits that other animals find toxic. Seeds from these fruits pass through the cassowary's digestive system and are released in its piles of droppings, known as scats. In scats, the seeds germinate and grow. As a result, this cassowary acts as an unknowing gardener to the rainforest, helping various plant species flourish where they could not otherwise grow.

Cassowaries are highly protective of their young and regularly attack if cornered. With claws 12 centimeters in length, most predators know better than to consider them prey. Cassowaries are very wary of one another, meeting only to mate. In the breeding season, the male builds a foamy mattress nest of leaves, upon which the female lays its eggs. It is the male, rather than the female, that sits on the eggs and raises the chicks.

HEIGHT: 130–180 cm

DIET: Fruits, seeds, fungus, insects, and small reptiles

FOUND IN: Rainforests across tropical regions of Australia, Papua New Guinea, and Indonesia

OSTRICHES, RHEAS, AND TINAMOUS

Closely related to emus, kiwis, and cassowaries, these groundbirds are the surviving members of a very ancient group of birds. Some scientists think that their prehistoric ancestors evolved to become flightless soon after the meteorite impact that killed the largest dinosaurs.

COMMON OSTRICH
(Struthio camelus)

Capable of reaching speeds of almost 50 miles per hour, ostriches are the fastest animal on two legs. Tendons in its legs act like rubber bands that catapult the body forward while running, meaning that each bounding stride of the common ostrich can be more than 5 meters apart. Its long, hooked claws act like spikes on a running shoe, providing the grip from which a single giant toe on each foot pushes off. Even ostrich chicks, within a month of hatching, can run at speeds of almost 30 miles an hour.

The 3-meter-wide nest of the common ostrich is filled with approximately twenty eggs, laid by more than one female. Compared to the size of the ostrich, these eggs are small. But compared to the eggs of other birds, ostrich eggs are the largest of all living birds. An ostrich egg is so big that it could fit twenty-four chicken's eggs inside it.

HEIGHT: 274 cm

DIET: Seeds, shrubs, grasses, fruits, and flowers

FOUND IN: Savannas and grasslands of Africa

GREATER RHEA
(Rhea americana)

When spooked, the greater rhea zigzags its way through the undergrowth, using its wings as sails to keep balance. By zigzagging while running, the rhea confuses its predators, especially cougars and jaguars.

Like the ostrich, the male greater rhea digs an immense hole in the ground that will become its nest. The male then encourages females to lay their eggs in the nest, which it protects. Successful males sometimes end up with sixty or more babies. The chicks hatch all at the same time, coordinating their hatching by making clicking and popping noises while they are still inside the egg.

HEIGHT: 170 cm

FOUND IN: Open grasslands throughout South America

DIET: Fruits, seeds, and leaves

GREAT TINAMOU
(Tinamus major)

Unlike ostriches and emus, their close cousins, tinamous can fly, but they do so clumsily, mostly to escape being eaten. Their predators include falcons and jaguars, as well as vampire bats, who sometimes visit at night to drink their blood.

Tinamou nests are often found in the clefts of tree roots, lightly covered in leaves. Like many flightless birds, the male tinamou looks after eggs from lots of different females. When hatched, the chicks grow quickly. Within as little as twenty-one days, they will be left to fend for themselves.

HEIGHT: 50 cm

FOUND IN: Dense rainforests throughout Central and South America

DIET: Berries, fruits, and seeds

SANDGROUSES

This group of ground-dwelling birds live in semi-deserts and savannas of Africa, the Middle East, and Asia. All sixteen species of sandgrouse are very well camouflaged. If spotted by predators, sandgrouses use strong flight muscles to launch into the air very quickly.

PIN-TAILED SANDGROUSE
(Pterocles alchata)

Water is a big part of the daily life of the pin-tailed sandgrouse. As the sun rises, flocks of up to 100 of them gather at watering holes, taking as much water as possible before moving across the dry landscape to search for seeds and leaf buds. They return in the evening to top up their water reserves as the sun sets.

Special feathers on the underside of the pin-tailed sandgrouse absorb water like a sponge. The male uses these feathers to collect water, which it carries back to its chicks to keep them hydrated.

LENGTH: 31–39 cm

DIET: Mostly seeds, with some leaf buds and flowers

FOUND IN: Stony semi-deserts throughout North Africa, the Middle East, and southern Europe

TIBETAN SANDGROUSE
(Syrrhaptes tibetanus)

Only at the hottest times of year does the Tibetan sandgrouse gather at watering holes to drink. For most of the year, living in cooler climates than other sandgrouse, it can collect enough water from its food (mostly green peas) to survive. It also drinks from hillside snow.

Unlike other birds, the toes of the Tibetan sandgrouse are covered in downy feathers that make its feet look like paws. Snug and cosy, these feathery feet remain warm when the sandgrouse walks through snow and frost.

LENGTH: 40 cm

DIET: Seeds, peas, and leaves

FOUND IN: Mountains of Central Asia, China, and the Himalayas

BUSTARDS

These large, ground-nesting birds live in grasslands throughout Europe and Asia, foraging on the floor for seeds and insects. In total, there are twenty-six species. In some parts of Asia, bustards are known as floricans or korhaans.

GREAT BUSTARD
(Otis tarda)

Weighing 100 times more than most birds, the great bustard is one of the heaviest flying birds in the world. Its weight means that, rather than fly away to avoid danger, many bustards prefer to run away on the ground. Some individuals can reach speeds of more than 30 miles per hour.

Ground-living is especially hard on bustard chicks. Four out of five of all great bustards are killed and eaten in their first year of life, often by foxes, wolves, and eagles.

HEIGHT: 100 cm

DIET: Plants, seeds, insects, and spiders

FOUND IN: Grasslands across parts of Europe and Asia

BENGAL FLORICAN
(Houbaropsis bengalensis)

With its feathers plumped up and head nodding up and down, the male Bengal florican struts its way through the undergrowth in spring. In special courtship flights, the male arches its legs in ballet-like fashion and gently floats down to the ground, hoping to catch the interests of nearby females.

Because many of its grassland habitats have been disturbed by humans, the Bengal florican has become one of the world's most endangered birds—fewer than 1,000 individuals remain. Scientists are working hard to make sure their grassland habitats are protected.

HEIGHT: 68 cm

DIET: Insects, seeds, fruits, and flowers

FOUND IN: Undisturbed grasslands throughout southern Asia

TOUCANS

Toucans have bright markings and long, colorful beaks that play a number of roles, from cracking open seeds and nuts to displaying to one another. Uniquely, this beak can also be used to get rid of body heat, keeping toucans cool. More than forty species are known, all living in the Americas.

TOCO TOUCAN
(Ramphastos toco)

For its size, the toco toucan has one of the longest beaks in the world. Strengthened with keratin, the same substance that human nails are made of, the beak is strong yet lightweight. Inside, a long tongue can be used to taste fleshy fruits such as figs. The tongue of the toco toucan is three times longer than a human's.

Being the largest of all toucans, the toco toucan is also a formidable predator that targets the nests of other birds, including blackbirds, flycatchers, and even birds that rival it for size, such as macaws and ibises.

LENGTH: 55–65 cm

DIET: Fruits and animals, particularly birds, lizards, and insects

FOUND IN: Tropical savannas across central and northern parts of South America

PLATE-BILLED MOUNTAIN TOUCAN
(Andigena laminirostris)

The courtship routine of the plate-billed mountain toucan is a show-stopping affair. Males and females leap and bound from branch to branch, showing off their colorful beak and feathers, while letting out loud donkey-like calls and bowing and bobbing their heads. As with other toucans, nests are mostly made in dead trees that have lots of holes in them.

When young plate-billed mountain toucans fledge the nest, the parent birds continue to feed them for three weeks. If the parents choose to breed again soon after, the youngsters are chased off their territory and urged to find a new one.

LENGTH: 46–51 cm

DIET: Mainly fruits

FOUND IN: Forests throughout the Andes mountain range in South America

LETTERED ARACARI

(Pteroglossus inscriptus)

The lettered aracari is so small that it could comfortably perch on a human hand. As well as feeding on fruits, this toucan regularly visits the forest floor to catch insects, especially army ants. It also eats the nestlings of rival hole-nesting birds, including pigeons and cardinals.

Being small means that the lettered aracari is at greater risk of being eaten than other toucans. Its predators include hawks, owls, and jaguars, as well as nest-raiding rainforest snakes such as the boa. It is very wary and alert for predators entering its patch.

LENGTH: 33–37 cm

DIET: Mainly fruits

FOUND IN: Forests throughout central regions of South America

KEEL-BILLED TOUCAN

(Ramphastos sulfuratus)

With a sensitive but strong beak, the keel-billed toucan can eat seeds and nuts that other toucans struggle to break open. Once grabbed with the beak, it splits seeds into pieces and then tosses them down the throat with a quick jerk of the head.

Back at the nest, the toughest and hardest parts of its meal are vomited up by the adult. These coughed-up seeds provide an extra layer of insulation for the hatchlings. The keel-billed toucan also brings small green leaves back to its nest. Some scientists think these leaves might work as a natural insect repellent.

LENGTH: 52–56 cm

DIET: Mostly fruits and seeds

FOUND IN: Rainforests from Southern Mexico to Venezuela and Colombia

WOODPECKERS, SAPSUCKERS, AND HONEYGUIDES

Woodpeckers and their relatives, the sapsuckers and honeyguides, nest in holes in tree trunks. Many species use a long, tough beak to rapidly peck out a drumming noise that can be heard from a long way away. In woodpeckers, this drumming sound performs the same function as a song.

GREAT SPOTTED WOODPECKER
(Dendrocopos major)

The great spotted woodpecker can strike its beak against a tree up to sixteen times a second. So that it doesn't get a headache, spongy sections in the skull absorb the shock, while special bones in the head act like a seatbelt for the brain, reducing the chance of bruising.

To avoid getting splinters in their airways while drumming, the great spotted woodpecker, like many woodpeckers, has small, stiff feathers that guard its nostrils.

LENGTH: 20–24 cm

DIET: Insects, snails, bird chicks, fruits, seeds, and carrion

FOUND IN: Woodlands throughout Europe, Asia, and northern Africa

NORTHERN FLICKER
(Colaptes auratus)

With a tongue able to stretch 5 centimeters out from the front of the beak, the northern flicker has one of the longest of all bird tongues for its size. If it were human-sized, this flicker's tongue would be longer than a toilet brush.

Like many woodpeckers, the northern flicker uses its sticky tongue to haul insects from out of tight spaces, such as cracks in tree bark or holes in the ground. Almost fifty per cent of a flicker's diet is made up of ants plucked from ant nests.

LENGTH: 28–31 cm

DIET: Insects, fruits, berries, seeds, and nuts

FOUND IN: Woodlands across North America

RED-BREASTED SAPSUCKER

(Sphyrapicus ruber)

The red-breasted sapsucker's tongue is not used for collecting insects. Instead, it is used for collecting sap, the sugary, gloopy liquid produced by trees. Up close, its long tongue is covered in scales, which help drag tree sap into
the mouth.

To find the freshest sap, the red-breasted sapsucker drills a neat row of holes on the side of a healthy tree and then waits for the sap to slowly flow out of the wounds. As sap drips out from these holes, insects are often attracted to the sweet smell. The red-breasted sapsucker eats these insects as a nutritious snack.

LENGTH: 20–22 cm

DIET: Sap and insects

FOUND IN: Forests throughout western North America

GREATER HONEYGUIDE

(Indicator indicator)

Honeyguides are one of the only birds in the world able to digest beeswax, which they find with a little help from human honey-gatherers. First, the greater honeyguide tries to attract a human's attention by hopping around while chattering. Then, once the person's attention is guaranteed, the honeyguide encourages the human toward a suitably large wild bees' nest it has seen in the forest.

At the buzzing nest, the human honey-gatherers use fire and smoke to calm the bees down while harvesting the honey. When they are finished, the hungry honeyguide feasts on the remains of the nest with its beak.

LENGTH: 19–20 cm

DIET: Beeswax, grubs, and eggs of honeybees

FOUND IN: Woodlands throughout central and southern Africa

HORNBILLS, HOOPOES, AND WOODHOOPOES

These striking birds are known for their long, curved beaks and their eye-catching colors and feather patterns. Spread across Africa, Asia, and some parts of Europe, seventy-seven species have so far been discovered and named. Each species has its own eye-catching technique for attracting mates.

KNOBBED HORNBILL
(Rhyticeros cassidix)

To avoid predators, the female knobbed hornbill lays eggs in a tree-trunk hole and then seals itself in place, making a locked door using its droppings as cement. In the weeks that follow, the male delivers food to the female through a small crack, which she feeds to the hatchlings. This strange nesting behavior protects the nest from rival hornbills, who regularly eat one another's chicks.

The hollow chamber on the top of the knobbed hornbill's beak (called a casque) works like an echo chamber, amplifying its gruff, barking call.

LENGTH: 70–80 cm

DIET: Fruits, birds, and insects

FOUND IN: Evergreen forests of some Indonesian islands

NORTHERN GROUND HORNBILL
(Bucorvus abyssinicus)

Ground hornbills eat much more meat than other hornbills. Snakes, frogs, insects, spiders, and even tortoises are regularly hunted, mostly by stalking prey on foot like a miniature *Tyrannosaurus rex*. A hungry northern ground hornbill can walk more than 7 miles in a day when searching for food.

The northern ground hornbill takes a long time to grow and reproduce. Unlike other birds, young ground hornbills remain near their parents for up to three years. Some pairs only produce a single chick once every nine years.

LENGTH: 90–100 cm

DIET: Animals and, less commonly, fruits, seeds, and nuts

FOUND IN: Savannas and scrublands of northern sub-Saharan Africa

EURASIAN HOOPOE
(Upupa epops)

With a long head-crest that can be flicked up and down, the Eurasian hoopoe is hard to miss. Its flexible crest helps scare away predators or rival hoopoes. When feeding, it plunges its sensitive beak into the ground and feels for insects, such as grubs or earwigs, squirming in the soil.

To kill larger insects, such as beetles or grasshoppers, the Eurasian hoopoe visits a favorite rock and bashes its prey against it again and again. This behavior helps breaks off insect body parts, such as wings and legs, that the hoopoe cannot digest.

LENGTH: 19–32 cm

DIET: Insects and their larvae

FOUND IN: Heathlands, savannas and grasslands throughout Europe, Asia, and northern Africa

GREEN WOODHOOPOE
(Phoeniculus purpureus)

The green woodhoopoe has a busy family life. Rather than leave to make a new nest, up to ten young hoopoes in each family hang around to help the mother raise more chicks. For weeks on end, they diligently feed the mother bird and her hungry chicks, helping the family to grow.

Guarding eggs from threats is especially important to the green woodhoopoe. These family groups angrily attack rival birds, particularly honeyguides, which, like cuckoos, sometimes try to sneak extra eggs into their nests.

LENGTH: 32–40 cm

DIET: Insects and their larvae

FOUND IN: Savannas and open woodlands of Africa

MEGAPODES, CHACHALACAS, AND CURASSOWS

These large, ground-dwelling fowl are part of a group known as the Galliformes. Largely flightless, they walk upon sturdy legs and often have sharp claws. Galliformes are a very old part of the bird family tree, which began around twenty million years after the extinction of the largest dinosaurs.

AUSTRALIAN BRUSHTURKEY
(Alectura lathami)

The tallest of all megapode birds is hard to miss. As well as its striking colors and neck decorations, the male Australian brushturkey also builds a giant mound of leaves that is twice the size of a king-size bed. It is within this mound that the female lays its eggs, which the male looks after.

Each day, to check their temperature, the male sticks its sensitive beak into the nest. If the eggs are too cold, the male adds more leaves. If the eggs are too warm, the male scrapes some leaves off.

LENGTH: 60–70 cm

DIET: Small animals and shoots, fruits, and berries

FOUND IN: Rainforests and scrublands across eastern Australia

MALEO
(Macrocephalon maleo)

The maleo is one of the only birds in the world not to sit on its eggs to keep them warm. Instead, its lays its eggs one at a time in sandy pits that are naturally heated by the midday sun or by underground lava chambers near volcanoes.

Once the egg hatches, the maleo chick climbs upward through the sand, sometimes digging a meter or more. When it reaches the surface, the mother is long gone, preparing another hole for its next egg. This technique, which is common among megapodes, means that mother and chick rarely meet.

LENGTH: 55 cm

DIET: Fruits, seeds, insects, and snails

FOUND IN: Forests on the Indonesian island of Sulawesi

RUFOUS-VENTED CHACHALACA

(Ortalis ruficauda)

Like the cuckoo and the chiffchaff, the chachalaca get its name from the noisy calls that pairs make when the sun rises. First, the male screams "CHA-CHA-LA-CA" and then, almost instantly, the female responds with a harsh "WATCH-A-LACK." Together, the calls help the pair stay connected.

The stomach of the rufous-vented chachalaca contains more soil and grit than other birds. This grit helps it grind up its fruit diet, so that it gets more energy from each meal. In total, this species is known to visit more than thirty different kinds of fruiting trees to find food.

LENGTH: 53–61 cm

DIET: Fruits

FOUND IN: Brushlands and forests in northern regions of South America

NOCTURNAL CURASSOW

(Nothocrax urumutum)

As the name suggests, the nocturnal curassow sings only at night. Two hours after sunset, on dark and moonless evenings, its ghostly song begins to ring out across the forest. Consisting of seven deep rumbling notes, this eerie noise carries up to a kilometer away.

Like other rainforest birds, the nocturnal curassow regularly visits special parts of the forest where the wet soil is particularly rich in minerals, especially calcium—an ingredient that birds need to produce their eggshells. Together, birds of many species, including parrots, remember where these spots are and revisit them many times.

LENGTH: 50–57.5 cm

DIET: Unknown, likely fruits

FOUND IN: Dense regions of the Amazon rainforest

PHEASANTS, QUAIL, AND GUINEAFOWL

These ground-nesting fowl are categorized as Galliformes and are closely related to megapodes, chachalacas, and curassows. These birds are strong runners and can escape predators by sprinting away rather than by flying. Males of these bird species often look very different from females.

INDIAN PEAFOWL
(Pavo cristatus)

With its dazzling eyespots and reflective green and blue feather patterns, the male Indian peafowl (commonly called a peacock) is hard to miss. In rainy seasons, male peacocks gather at special locations in the forest where females, one by one, inspect them. The more eyespots the feathers have, the better the male's chances of fathering chicks. For added effect when displaying, the peacock vibrates its long feathers to make a hypnotic whirring noise.

The male's elaborate, yet cumbersome, feathers make escaping predators difficult and so, in the breeding season, peacocks are regularly eaten by leopards, large eagles, and owls. Using their claws, tigers have been known to pin them to the floor by the tail feathers. Some scientists think that predators may be one reason why the female Indian peafowl has such an interest in long feathers and eyespots. The argument goes that if peacocks can survive and prosper with such burdensome feathers, they are surely fit and healthy enough to father chicks.

WINGSPAN: 80–130 cm

DIET: Seeds, fruits, insects, worms, fruits, small mammals, frogs, lizards, and small snakes

FOUND IN: Forests across India

VULTURINE GUINEAFOWL
(Acryllium vulturinum)

Named for its featherless, vulture-like head, the vulturine guineafowl plays an important role in forest ecosystems by eating blood-sucking ticks and disease-carrying flies. Using its broad beak, it can also pluck maggots from the bodies of dead animals.

Like other guineafowl, the vulturine guineafowl also tracks groups of monkeys, picking at seeds in their droppings and foraging for insects and fruits that they knock to the floor as they move through the forest canopy. Often, the vulturine guineafowl moves in noisy groups of twenty or more, whose "chink-chink-chink-chink-chink" calls ring through the forest.

LENGTH: 60–72 cm

FOUND IN: Dry grasslands of northeast Africa

DIET: Seeds, berries, fruits, insects, spiders, and scorpions

WILD TURKEY
(Meleagris gallopavo)

The wild turkey is well known for its impressive vocal skills. Its calls include purring notes, clucking, whining screams, yelps, and, strangest of all, an ultrasonic drumming sound made by rattling air in a special sac deep in its chest. The celebrated "gobble" call, which males use to impress females, can travel 2 kilometers through the forest.

Unlike many Galliformes, the wild turkey is a strong flier that can move more than 400 meters through the air to escape predators.

LENGTH: 76–125 cm

FOUND IN: Forests across North America, sometimes straying into pastures, fields, and marshlands

DIET: Seeds, berries, nuts, fruits, insects, and spiders

BARN OWLS

With heart-shaped, feathery faces that funnel sounds toward the ears, barn owls differ from other birds of prey. Barn owls live in a variety of habitats, from deserts to forests. In total, twenty species have been discovered. Many are very secretive indeed.

COMMON BARN OWL
(Tyto alba)

Living on every continent except Antarctica, the common barn owl is one of the most widespread of all owls. The secret to its success is its adaptability. Barn owls thrive in woodlands, grasslands, and farmlands, sometimes catching three or four mice each night. In some parts of the world, the barn owl hunts in the day as well as the night.

Unlike other owls, the barn owl does not hoot. Instead, it produces an eerie, haunting screech.

LENGTH: 33–35 cm

FOUND IN: Open habitats across the world

DIET: Rats, mice, voles, and other rodents

RED OWL
(Tyto soumagnei)

The red owl is the most mysterious of all barn owls. Until thirty years ago, scientists had not seen one for centuries and presumed it was extinct.

Unlike other barn owls, which nest in tree holes and old buildings, the red owl makes its nest in rocky ledges or caves, which are harder for scientists to find. To locate red owl nests, scientists listen out for its high-pitched screeching calls, which differ slightly from those of other barn owls.

LENGTH: 27–30 cm

FOUND IN: Deciduous and evergreen forests of Madagascar

DIET: Lizards, including geckos, as well as rodents

ORIENTAL BAY-OWL
(Phodilus badius)

There are few parents better than the Oriental bay-owl. For more than forty days, both male and female hunt for their chicks, providing them with an almost never-ending supply of lizards, frogs, rats, and mice to eat.

When hunting, the Oriental bay-owl sits on a perch and scans its surroundings for signs of prey. If food is spotted, its short wings allow it to fly stealthily through the undergrowth until its claws and beak are within striking distance of its prey.

LENGTH: 23–29 cm

DIET: Birds, snakes, large spiders, insects, and rodents, including rats and mice

FOUND IN: Woodlands and swamps throughout China, Nepal, Southeast Asia, and Australia

SOOTY OWL
(Tyto tenebricosa)

Like all barn owls, the sooty owl rarely strays from its home territory. These noisy owls are easiest to hear near the nest. Their calls include shrieks, twittering melodies, and long descending notes that are known as "falling bombs" to the scientists who study them.

The sooty owl hunts marsupial (pouched) mammals, including bandicoots and possums. Its large eyes help it scan the forest floor for movement or spot the tell-tale gliding leaps of some marsupials, such as the sugar glider, between the trees.

LENGTH: 37–50 cm

DIET: Marsupials, as well as birds, bats, and large insects

FOUND IN: Mountain rainforests of southeastern Australia and New Guinea

TRUE OWLS

True owls have circle-shaped patches of feathers around the eyes. This differs from barn owls, whose faces are more heart-shaped. True owls also have yellow or orange eyes and, in some species, special tufts of feathers near the ears. Living all over the world, more than 200 species of these mostly nocturnal birds of prey are known.

GREAT GRAY OWL
(Strix nebulosa)

Standing twice as tall as a house cat, the great gray owl is one of the largest of all owls. When hunting at night, it often sits on a fence post and listens out for the sounds of rats or mice moving through the undergrowth. The circular patches of feathers on its face (known as facial disks) focus sounds toward the ears.

Unlike most other owls, the great gray owl regularly dives into snow to grab prey hiding in burrows beneath the surface. Its ears are so sensitive that it can hear small mammals moving beneath 60 centimeters or more of snow.

LENGTH: 61–84 cm

DIET: Rodents, especially lemmngs, rats, and mice

FOUND IN: Coniferous forests across North America and northern Eurasia

SNOWY OWL
(Bubo scandiacus)

The snowy owl has the best insulation of any bird, except for penguins. Its tightly packed feathers mean it can withstand temperatures of more than -50 °C with no obvious discomfort. Because digesting food generates body heat, the snowy owl needs to eat six or seven meals a day to stay alive.

The snowy owl is as much a daytime hunter as it is nocturnal. It changes its hunting patterns according to the availability of its food, which mostly consists of mouse-like rodents known as lemmings.

LENGTH: 53–66 cm

FOUND IN: Arctic tundra

DIET: Small mammals, mostly lemmings

BURROWING OWL
(Athene cunicularia)

As the name suggests, the burrowing owl nests in long burrows, often made by ground squirrels. If disturbed in its hole, this owl makes a rattling and hissing sound that mimics an angry rattlesnake. This makes predators think twice about entering.

Unlike other owls, the burrowing owl has evolved long legs that allow it to sprint across the floor when chasing prey. In flight, the burrowing owl can also catch large flying insects and bats. It regularly hunts underneath streetlights, where these animals sometimes gather at night.

LENGTH: 19–25 cm

DIET: Mostly insects, birds, and small mammals

FOUND IN: Grasslands and deserts throughout North and South America

BUFFY FISH OWL
(Ketupa ketupu)

Like a fish-eating eagle, the buffy fish owl strikes at fish just below the surface of the water using its long, clawed toes. As well as eating fish, this owl has also been known to eat snakes, frogs, and even baby crocodiles.

The nest of the buffy fish owl can be very messy. After eating, it vomits up indigestible parts of its meal in the nest and does little to clear up the mess. This differs from other owls, who cough up tidy pellets that are quickly and cleanly removed from the nest.

LENGTH: 40–48 cm

DIET: Mostly fish, crabs, frogs, small reptiles, and birds

FOUND IN: Tropical forests and wetlands throughout Southeast Asia

COCKATOOS

Cockatoos are a family of parrots with a crest on the head that can be flicked upward. This crest helps cockatoos communicate with one another. Cockatoos are very social and intelligent. In total, twenty-one species are known, mostly found in Australasia.

GALAH
(Eolophus roseicapilla)

The galah regularly gathers in noisy flocks of more than 1,000 individuals, which scour dry grasslands looking for seeds and leaves. With beaks as strong as a pair of pliers, some large flocks of galahs have been known to kill trees by stripping them entirely of their leaves and bark.

Like other cockatoos, the galah can live for a long time. Provided it can avoid predators such as eagles and peregrine falcons, the galah can live for twenty years or more in the wild, and some galahs in captivity have lived more than seventy years.

LENGTH: 34–38 cm

FOUND IN: Australia, except for in dense forests

DIET: Seeds, bark, and leaves

PALM COCKATOO
(Probosciger aterrimus)

The palm cockatoo is the only bird in the world to use tools to help show off to a mate. During the breeding season, the male palm cockatoo carefully prepares a hard piece of wood, creating a drumstick that can be rattled against tree trunks to make an eerie knocking sound that travels far through the forest.

The palm cockatoo nests in holes in trees that have been hollowed out by forest fires or by termites or other insects. Here, it lays a single egg, once every two years.

LENGTH: 51–64 cm

DIET: Fruits and nuts

FOUND IN: Rainforests and woodlands of New Guinea and northern Australia

SULFUR-CRESTED COCKATOO
(Cacatua galerita)

In cities, sulfur-crested cockatoos can learn new techniques to open garbage cans so that they can feed on human food waste. Regularly, cockatoos of this species observe one another's techniques and repeat them on their own. This form of learning (called horizontal learning) is rare among birds.

When sulfur-crested cockatoos eat seeds on the floor, one cockatoo will always stand guard in a nearby tree. If a predator is spotted, a single alarm call is all it takes for the flock to scatter into the air.

LENGTH: 50 cm

DIET: Grass, seeds, nuts, and insects

FOUND IN: Forests and woodlands throughout Australia, New Guinea, and nearby islands

COCKATIEL
(Nymphicus hollandicus)

What the cockatiel lacks in size, it makes up for in character. Its long, flexible head-crest is used to communicate emotions to other members of the flock. When startled or excited, the crest is held upright like a flag. When angry, the cockatiel flattens its crest closer to its head. By reading one another's crests, cockatiels can ease tension within the group, avoiding costly physical fights and scuffles.

The cockatiel nests in holes in old tree trunks. This is the only cockatoo able to breed within almost a year of hatching out of its egg.

LENGTH: 29–33 cm

DIET: Seeds

FOUND IN: Wetlands and scrublands of Australia

LORIES AND LORIKEETS, BUDGERIGARS, AND FIG PARROTS

This collection of small and colorful parrots is found throughout Southeast Asia and Oceania. Noisy, intelligent, and highly social, they use a sharp, hooked beak to open seeds, fruits, and flowers. Because their diet changes from season to season, many of these parrots travel long distances to find food each year.

RAINBOW LORIKEET
(Trichoglossus moluccanus)

In its daily search for flower nectar and fruits, the rainbow lorikeet can move 60 miles or more. This parrot has even been known to raid the half-opened fruits, including mangoes, left behind by fruit bats.

As with other lorikeets, the tongue of the rainbow lorikeet is shaped like a brush at the tip. This special tongue is used to scrape pollen and nectar from flowers. As it moves from flower to flower, the rainbow lorikeet carries pollen around to other plants. Without this precious pollen, coconut trees, in particular, would struggle to grow.

LENGTH: 25–30 cm

DIET: Fruits, pollen, and nectar

FOUND IN: Rainforests and wooded areas across eastern Australia

SCALY-BREASTED LORIKEET
(Trichoglossus chlorolepidotus)

The dappled, reflective feathers of the scaly-breasted lorikeet help it camouflage itself among sunlit leaves and branches, safe from the eyes of predators like peregrine falcons and kites. To keep safe from these predators while flying, this lorikeet often sticks close to it neighbors, guided by a continuous metallic screeching call.

As well as eating nectar, the scaly-breasted lorikeet also eats fruit. This means that, at certain times of the year when other food is scarce, orchards and farms can become a life-saving resource for them.

LENGTH: 23 cm

DIET: Nectar, pollen, fruits, and, occasionally, insects

FOUND IN: Woodlands and forests across eastern Australia

BUDGERIGAR
(Melopsittacus undulatus)

To keep one another alive during periods of drought, the budgerigar can regurgitate (vomit) half-digested seeds into the mouth of others in its flock. Individuals in a flock also look after one another in other ways, including by preening each other's feathers to keep them clean.

When it is dry for long periods, budgerigars move around in noisy flocks that look for ripe grasses just about to produce their nutritious seeds. Only when rains arrive do the budgerigars begin making a nest, often searching for hollow logs and tree stumps that remain dry.

LENGTH: 17–18 cm

DIET: Grass seeds

FOUND IN: Forests, grasslands, and farmlands across Australia

SCARLET-CHEEKED FIG PARROT
(Psittaculirostris edwardsii)

The scarlet-cheeked fig parrot is a sociable bird that is often found feeding on fruit trees alongside pigeons, honeyeaters, and starlings. This parrot is especially fond of figs infested with tiny wasp grubs. These grubs provide the scarlet-cheeked fig parrot with an extra source of nutrition.

As with many fig parrots, the scarlet-cheeked fig parrot hides its nest in tiny holes and crevices found in the treetops. High up and out of reach, its nests are so difficult to see that scientists know very little about the nesting behavior of this species.

LENGTH: 18 cm

DIET: Fig fruits

FOUND IN: Forests across northern New Guinea

NEW ZEALAND PARROTS

The islands of New Zealand are home to an ancient group of parrots known as the Strigopidae. According to the family tree of birds, these parrots split from other parrots at around the time of dinosaurs. Three species survive today: One in the mountains, one in the treetops, and one on the ground.

KEA
(Nestor notabilis)

This large, intelligent mountain parrot has one of the most varied diets of all birds. As well as eating forty kinds of plants, seeds and fruits, the kea eats caterpillars and grubs and even raids the nests of other birds to eat their chicks.

This adaptable New Zealand parrot also chews on the bones of dead animals and is well known for snacking on human garbage, often stolen from trashcans. The kea has no fear of people and often investigates backpacks, handbags, and other human belongings, in its daily search for food.

LENGTH: 48 cm

DIET: Varied animals and plants

FOUND IN: Mountainous regions of South Island, New Zealand

KĀKĀ
(Nestor meridionalis)

With its long and sturdy beak, the New Zealand kākā strips wood from trees to get at sugary sap that gathers beneath the bark. It has a long, bristly tongue that can also be used to scrape nectar from flowers or to obtain sugary liquid, known as honeydew, produced by tiny, aphid-like insects.

At dawn and dusk, the kākā gathers in large, noisy flocks. Its call is a grating "krraah" mixed with a series of trembling whistles.

LENGTH: 45 cm

DIET: Fruits, seeds, nectar, sap, and insects

FOUND IN: Large, forested areas of South Island, New Zealand

KĀKĀPŌ

(Strigops habroptila)

There is no more distinctive bird on Earth than the kākāpō: A giant, nocturnal, flightless, herbivorous parrot. This toddler-sized parrot jogs around the forest, searching out plants as their fruits ripen.

The kākāpō is especially renowned for its strange breeding behavior. Every five years or so, when a certain type of tree begins to bear fruit, males construct special "courts" from high on the mountainside. Each bowl-shaped court resembles a satellite dish. When singing in the middle of this construction, the kākāpō's booming calls are broadcast far and wide, for eight hours at a time. These songs can carry on the wind for almost 5 kilometers.

In the last century, the introduction of cats, rats, and stoats to remote islands off New Zealand has seen the number of kākāpō drop sharply. At the current time, less than 250 individuals are left in the wild. Scientists are working hard to find new predator-free habitats in which the kākāpō might one day thrive.

LENGTH: 64 cm

DIET: Plants

FOUND IN: Remote forests and scrublands on New Zealand's Kapiti Island, Codfish Island, and Little Barrier Island

PARROTS

"True" parrots include macaws, parakeets, and parrotlets. Known for their bright colors and strong beaks, many of these parrots live in South America and Africa. They include, among their numbers, some of the most intelligent of all birds. Some parrots are thought to be as clever as chimpanzees.

HYACINTH MACAW
(Anodorhynchus hyacinthinus)

With a length of more than a meter, the hyacinth macaw is the largest of all flying parrots. Its sturdy beak can be used to crack open hard nuts that other birds avoid, like coconuts and Brazil nuts. A strong, bony tongue, is used to tease open cracks in the shell of the nut, to get to the nutritious insides.

Like many parrots, the hyacinth macaw has been hunted for centuries for its colorful feathers. Though scientists are working hard to protect its habitats, the species remains close to extinction.

LENGTH: 100 cm

DIET: Palm nuts and, occasionally, fruits

FOUND IN: Forests, savannas, and dry woodlands throughout Brazil, Paraguay, and Bolivia

SCARLET MACAW
(Ara macao)

During the breeding season, the sharp beak of the scarlet macaw becomes a formidable weapon. It uses its beak to chase away predators or rivals eager to kill its hatchlings, which it hides in a nest in the crevice of a tree. Even with this round-the-clock care, only fifty per cent of scarlet macaw hatchlings survive. Many are eaten by nest-raiding predators, especially toucans.

Like many parrots, the scarlet macaw has a long lifespan, with some individuals living in the wild for forty or fifty years. This extended lifespan means that, provided there are more good years than bad, macaws can guarantee lots of offspring.

LENGTH: 84–89 cm

DIET: Fruits, seeds, and bark

FOUND IN: The Amazon rainforest

MONK PARAKEET
(Myiopsitta monachus)

The monk parakeet avoids tree holes, which most parrots prefer for their nests. Instead, this parakeet builds messy nests in branches, made up of multiple layers of carefully trimmed sticks. Often, once a single nest is built, other pairs of monk parakeets add their own nest constructions to it. Combined, these "parakeet apartments," built high in the treetops, can become as big as a car.

In some parts of the world, monk parakeets have been known to build their large nests on electrical powerlines and power stations, causing blackouts and, occasionally, fires.

LENGTH: 29 cm

DIET: Seeds, leaf buds, fruits, berries, and nuts

FOUND IN: Grasslands and dry woodlands throughout South America, North America, and Europe

GRAY PARROT
(Psittacus erithacus)

The gray parrot is one of the most chatty of all birds. In the wild, it has been found to use more than 200 calls, some of which mimic other birds and, occasionally, even bats. Often, when they are young, individuals learn these calls from their parents or from others in their busy flocks.

In captivity, the gray parrot can learn quickly from humans. Some gray parrots have been shown to count or do simple mathematical equations. Others have shown an understanding of more than 100 human words and can use them to describe objects, colors, and shapes.

LENGTH: 33 cm

DIET: Fruits, seeds, flowers, and buds

FOUND IN: Dense forests across Central Africa

BULBULS

Bulbuls are a family of medium-sized birds that fit within the group of birds known as perching birds (or passerines). In total, 166 species of bulbul are known. They live throughout Africa, Europe, and Asia.

RED-WHISKERED BULBUL
(Pycnonotus jocosus)

Each morning, the red-whiskered bulbul delivers a high-pitched "KINK-A-JOO!" call into the sky. As with most perching birds, singing early in the day, when the air is cooler and clearer, helps its calls travel further through the forest.

In recent years, the red-whiskered bulbul has been introduced, sometimes accidentally, to other parts of the world, including Australia and parts of the USA. This can be a problem, because their droppings often contain undigested seeds, which cause weeds to spread to places they shouldn't normally be.

LENGTH: 17–23 cm

DIET: Fruits, nectar, and insects

FOUND IN: Native to woodlands, shrublands, and farmlands across Asia

LIGHT-VENTED BULBUL
(Pycnonotus sinensis)

In parts of China, the light-vented bulbul is one of the most common neighborhood birds. Its success is partly because of its ability to remember where berries and other fruits are found each season. The light-vented bulbul is also brave. Individuals regularly lose their fear of people and learn to feed on scraps left accidentally near houses or roads.

In the last thirty years, because of climate change, the light-vented bulbul has moved further north across China, exploring new habitats where once it was too cold to thrive.

LENGTH: 18–19 cm

DIET: Fruits, seeds, and insects

FOUND IN: Wooded habitats and gardens across Asia

SATINBIRDS

With their colorful feathers and decorated crests, satinbirds were once thought to be closely related to birds of paradise. Recent studies suggest they are actually more closely related to berrypeckers. This perching bird family contains just four species, which all live in the mountain forests of New Guinea.

CRESTED SATINBIRD
(Cnemophilus macgregorii)

Though it does not sing, the crested satinbird produces loud hisses and clicking sounds that may serve as a warning to others to stay well away. Throughout the day, the male crested satinbird is very watchful of rivals. Much of its time is spent patrolling its 200-square-meter territory.

At the center of its patch is the nest, built entirely by the female. About the width of a dinner plate, the dome-shaped nest is covered in green mosses and ferns to keep it well hidden. Inside, the nest is lined exclusively with green and yellow stems collected from orchids.

LENGTH: 24 cm

DIET: Fruits

FOUND IN: Mountain forests of eastern and southeastern New Guinea

YELLOW-BREASTED SATINBIRD
(Loboparadisea sericea)

Without knowing it, the yellow-breasted satinbird helps the forest grow. Like other satinbirds, it feeds by gently plucking ripe fruits and berries and swallowing them whole. Many seeds from its diet pass through the bird's gut and come out in its droppings, where they fall to the ground and begin to grow into new plants.

The yellow-breasted satinbird is very secretive. Sightings of adult birds are very rare, though there have been occasional reports of small flocks gathering in fruiting trees. Scientists are yet to see or study its nest.

LENGTH: 17 cm

DIET: Fruits and, occasionally, insects

FOUND IN: Scattered mountain forests of New Guinea

AUSTRALASIAN ROBINS

This small group of Australasian birds is not closely related to the red-breasted robins of Europe. In total, fifty-one species are known, each with a large, round head and a short, straight bill used to catch insects. Most Australasian robins hunt using a "perch-and-pounce" method of attack.

SCARLET ROBIN
(Petroica boodang)

The eye-catching colors of the scarlet robin are a warning that tells rival robins to keep away. As with many birds, these colors are also used in springtime to help individuals show off to potential breeding partners—the redder the breast, the healthier and more attractive the mate.

As with many Australasian robins, the scarlet robin changes its hunting habits throughout the year. In spring and summer, it picks at insects hiding deep within tree bark; in winter, it pecks at the forest floor searching for spiders.

WINGSPAN: 20.5 cm

DIET: Insects and spiders

FOUND IN: Eucalyptus woodlands and forests across Australia

WHITE-BREASTED ROBIN
(Eopsaltria georgiana)

What the white-breasted robin lacks in color, it makes up for in character. These robins form noisy family groups, which work together to build nests in which the parent birds will lay more eggs. Often, it is the sons that remain helpers at the family nest for longest, sometimes for a year or more.

White-breasted robins make their cup-shaped nests out of dry grass and bark, bound together with spiderwebs.

WINGSPAN: 22–25 cm

DIET: Insects and spiders

FOUND IN: Dense scrublands and forests across western Australia

AUSTRALASIAN MUDNESTERS

This tiny group of perching birds contains just two species, both living in dry scrublands and forests in eastern Australia, as well as in gardens and parks. As the name suggests, these birds make bowl-shaped nests out of mud, which can take many days to construct.

WHITE-WINGED CHOUGH
(Corcorax melanorhamphos)

In large and noisy family groups, sometimes containing twenty individuals or more, the white-winged chough spends its day, hopping through the undergrowth searching for food. Only when disturbed by a predator does this species take to the air, finding a nearby branch to see away the threat.

The bigger the group, the greater the chance each individual has of finding food. This leads some small family groups to "kidnap" the fledglings of their rivals, to make their families as big as possible.

WINGSPAN: 65 cm

DIET: Insects, fruits, seeds, and plant shoots

FOUND IN: Dry woodlands throughout southern and eastern Australia

APOSTLEBIRD
(Struthidea cinerea)

Apostlebird flocks go by a variety of nicknames, including "happy jacks" or "happy families." This is because, like the white-winged chough, this Australian mudnester moves around in noisy family groups.

Young members of the family support the parent birds in making their cup-shaped nest, constructed 7 or 8 meters above ground at the base of a tree branch. Once dry, these cement-like nests can be used again and again, year after year. Other birds regularly seek out abandoned apostlebird nests and take the chance to use them for their own eggs.

LENGTH: 29–33 cm

FOUND IN: Dry woodlands across eastern Australia

DIET: Mostly insects, spiders, and seeds

BIRDS OF PARADISE

The feathers of the so-called "birds of paradise" are among the most colorful and decorated of all birds. This family, which contains forty-five species, is found mostly across Indonesia, Papua New Guinea, and eastern Australia.

RAGGIANA BIRD-OF-PARADISE
(Paradisaea raggiana)

The male Raggiana bird-of paradise wants as many females as possible to see its long tail feathers and bright colors. To make this happen, males gather together in so-called "leks." Leks are special meeting places where females can take time to inspect the quality of each male on show before mating.

As well as eating insects, the Raggiana bird-of-paradise also eats fruit. The seeds from the fruit pass through the bird's digestive system and are released in its droppings. These seeds grow into new fruit trees, helping the forest ecosystem flourish.

LENGTH: 33–34 cm, plus 60-cm tail feathers

FOUND IN: Tropical forests of eastern New Guinea

DIET: Fruits, insects, and spiders

KING BIRD-OF-PARADISE
(Cicinnurus regius)

To draw as much attention to itself as possible, the male king bird-of-paradise is a masterful mover. As well as dancing and strutting, it is even able to dangle head-first off its branch and swing its feathers back and forth like a pendulum on a clock.

Like other birds of paradise, its shimmering feather colors change depending on the direction that light shines down on them. This happens because microscopic notches (called barbules) at the edge of each feather scatter light in lots of directions at once.

LENGTH: 16–19 cm, not including 15-cm tail feathers

FOUND IN: Lowland forests of mainland New Guinea and nearby islands

DIET: Fruits, insects, and spiders

WILSON'S BIRD-OF-PARADISE
(Diphyllodes respublica)

The male Wilson's bird-of-paradise spends hours clearing away twigs and dead leaves from its territory, creating a stage that females can see from all around. From here, the male dances to and fro, while flexing a fluorescent green collar that females watch with interest.

As with all birds of paradise, the more eye-catching the male, the more interested females become. This is because females use color as a way to judge how healthy a potential mate might be. The healthier the mate, the best chance of healthy chicks.

LENGTH: 16 cm, not including 5-cm tail feathers

FOUND IN: Rainforests of Waigeo and Batanta Islands off West Papua

DIET: Fruits, insects, and spiders

BLACK SICKLEBILL
(Epimachus fastosus)

The black sicklebill's scientific name means "equipped for battle," so called because its calls sound like the firing of a gun. During the breeding season, it can also produce a woodpecker-like drumming noise by rubbing the shafts of its feathers against one another.

When displaying to a female, the black sicklebill pulls up two special flaps on the sides of its body. This causes its silhouette to transform into a strange, comet-shaped blob. Poised like this, the male moves gently up and down in robotic fashion.

LENGTH: 55–63 cm, not including 47-cm tail feathers

FOUND IN: Mountain forests of New Guinea

DIET: Fruits, insects, and spiders

PARROTS AND ALLIES | PERCHING BIRDS | PIGEONS AND DOVES | TUNNEL-NESTERS | WATERBIRDS | FORGOTTEN BIRDS

MAGNIFICENT RIFLEBIRD
(Ptiloris magnificus)

On its treetop stage, the male magnificent riflebird holds open its wings, sways its body right and left and lashes its head from side to side expressively, like a ballet dancer. The female joins in the dance, holding her body upright in front of his. As they court, the male's feathers produce a whooshing sound, which the female uses, as well as color, to judge the male's quality.

The black feathers of the magnificent riflebird are among the darkest colors in nature. They help the green and blue markings on its face stand out better. The intense contrast effect happens because the microscopic feather edges (barbules) that normally give birds of paradise their shiny colors are spiky instead of flat. This spikiness traps nearly all of the light received from the sun and stops it from reflecting. One day, scientists hope to make microscopic structures like these artificially in laboratories to improve technologies like solar panels and telescopes.

LENGTH: 28–34 cm

DIET: Fruits, insects, and spiders

FOUND IN: Lowland rainforests of western New Guinea and the northernmost tip of Australia

BOWERBIRDS

Bowerbirds are celebrated for the unique courtship behavior. Males build special structures (called bowers), which they surround with brightly colored objects to impress females. There are twenty-seven species of bowerbird, all living in New Guinea and Australia.

SATIN BOWERBIRD
(Ptilonorhynchus violaceus)

Berries, flowers, snail shells, and human garbage, including drinking straws and clothes pegs, are just some of the items that the satin bowerbird uses to decorate its bower. Blue items are especially favored. Scientists think this is because blue colors make the satin bowerbird's feathers stand out more.

This bowerbird is a talented mimic, capable of copying the calls of many of the birds that share its forest habitat. Males that are good mimics are especially attractive to females.

LENGTH: 32–33 cm

DIET: Fruits, leaves, and seeds

FOUND IN: Rainforests and woodlands of eastern Australia

VOGELKOP BOWERBIRD
(Amblyornis inornata)

With a bower as big as a bathtub, the Vogelkop bowerbird builds one of the largest of all bowers. Built like a hut, it has an entrance-way, often propped open with sticks, and is decorated with novel objects. It even has a front lawn.

When nesting, the female Vogelkop bowerbird also demonstrates keen engineering skills. On top of a loose mesh of carefully selected sticks, she lays a carpet of leaves, ferns, and carefully snipped vine tendrils, upon which she lays a single egg.

LENGTH: 25 cm

DIET: Fruits, leaves, seeds, and, occasionally, insects

FOUND IN: Mountain forests of West Papua, New Guinea

CISTICOLAS

There are 160 species of the secretive perching birds known as cisticolas. Hidden in the undergrowth and very hard to spot, the presence of these insect-eating birds is often only given away by their shrill calls or warbling songs.

ZITTING CISTICOLA
(Cisticola juncidis)

Pairs of zitting cisticolas build their nest suspended in dense grasses, woven with leaves and held together with silk collected from spiderwebs. On the top of the nest, the pair build a canopy-like structure, like the roof of a tent. This camouflages the nest from birds of prey hovering above.

The strange "zitting" call that this species makes often occurs mid-flight, while it performs its zig-zagging aerial dance. Some say that the call sounds like the snipping of scissors.

LENGTH: 10–12 cm

DIET: Insects

FOUND IN: Grasslands throughout Europe, Africa, southern Asia, and northern Australia

GOLDEN-HEADED CISTICOLA
(Cisticola exilis)

Occupying a region thirty-seven million square kilometers in size, the golden-headed cisticola is a very successful species. Provided there is long grass in which to hunt insects and make its nests, it can live in a variety of habitats. These habitats include swamps and wetlands, savannas, and dry scrublands.

Should wildfires scorch their nesting areas, the golden-headed cisticola has even been known to take temporary refuge in woodlands and forests. In wetland areas, the golden-headed cisticola is especially fond of eating small slugs.

LENGTH: 9–11 cm

DIET: Insects and slugs

FOUND IN: Numerous grassy habitats across Asia and Australia

CRICKET LONGTAIL
(Spiloptila clamans)

The cricket longtail gets its name from its call, which sounds like a cricket or grasshopper churring. Often these calls are made by individuals as they flock together in small groups, while flying from tree to tree. Known as contact calls, these special sounds act like a roll-call in a school classroom, helping the group stay together at all times.

In their pursuit of insects, groups of cricket longtails occasionally stray into dry and dusty deserts. Here, they live happily provided there are tufts of grass to keep them shaded from the hot sun.

LENGTH: 11–12 cm

DIET: Insects

FOUND IN: Thorny scrublands across central Africa

GRAY-CAPPED WARBLER
(Eminia lepida)

Many birds steer well clear of venomous spiders and praying mantises, but not the gray-capped warbler. This broad-bodied cisticola regularly includes these animals in its diet, pulling them to pieces with its strong, robust beak.

The gray-capped warbler also finds food by inspecting cracks in tree bark for beetle grubs and running its beak through the gaps within curled-up leaves where caterpillars can often be found. This feeding technique, which many cisticolas use, is called gleaning.

LENGTH: 15 cm

DIET: Insects, spiders, and millipedes

FOUND IN: Tropical shrublands across Africa, including Kenya, Tanzania, and Uganda

COTINGAS

This large group of fruit-eating birds lives in the forests of Central and South America. Cotingas have broad, slightly hooked beaks and rounded wings. Like birds of paradise, male cotingas can be very colorful, showing off to nearby females from special perches.

ANDEAN COCK-OF-THE-ROCK
(Rupicola peruvianus)

The Andean cock-of-the-rock gets its name from the male's habit of standing on rocks during the breeding season to display to females. This display involves bobbing and hopping, along with lots of squawking and grunting calls.

To maintain its dazzling colors, the Andean cock-of-the-rock requires a mix of high-energy foods. As well as eating fruits, individuals occasionally track colonies of army ants through the forest, catching and eating insects and spiders as they flee from the invading ants.

LENGTH: 32 cm

DIET: Mostly fruits, along with occasional insects, frogs, and small reptiles and mammals

FOUND IN: Forests throughout the Andes mountain range

POMPADOUR COTINGA
(Xipholena punicea)

Very little is known about this elusive rainforest cotinga because it lives high up in the rainforest canopy. Its tough beak and wide mouth suggests that it can swallow both fruits and small animals, including lizards.

The courtship behavior of the pompadour cotinga has only been observed a few times by scientists. Male cotingas gather together and chase one another excitedly, challenging one another in combat. Quietly, the female observes from below. To learn more about mysterious Amazonian cotingas like this, scientists hope to use special cranes or drones that can fly through the treetops.

LENGTH: 20 cm

DIET: Fruits and animals, including insects and lizards

FOUND IN: The Amazon rainforest

WHITE BELLBIRD
(*Procnias albus*)

The white bellbird is the world's loudest bird. At 125 decibels, its calls are more piercing than a chainsaw and, up close, more deafening than a rock concert. The call is produced by the male. At first, the male sings into the sky and then, halfway through the song, it swivels its body to fire the sound directly toward the female. This sonic blast is so loud that, at close quarters, it may damage the female's hearing.

Like all perching birds, the white bellbird has a complex voice box known as a syrinx. The syrinx contains lots of muscles and fleshy material, through which air is squeezed from the lungs. As the muscles pull the syrinx in different ways, a range of complex sounds is produced.

The male bellbird has a fleshy mustache that hangs down beside its beak. This structure, which males use to impress females, is known as a wattle.

LENGTH: 27–29 cm

DIET: Fruits

FOUND IN: Tropical and subtropical rainforests through many parts of South America

CROWS, RAVENS, AND JAYS

These clever, quick, and noisy perching birds form a group known as corvids. Many corvids can use simple tools, like sharp sticks, to help them find prey. Some can even recognize themselves in a mirror.

COMMON RAVEN
(Corvus corax)

Found across the northern hemisphere, the common raven is adaptable, wily, and cunning. Its tough beak can be put to a variety of tasks, from pulling meat off dead animals and cracking nuts, to tenderly plucking berries from trees.

Often the common raven works in pairs. Ravens pair up with a mate, spending their life together defending a territory and, each spring, raising chicks. In the wild, some ravens can live almost twenty-five years.

WINGSPAN: 120–150 cm

DIET: Carrion, insects, berries, fruits, human garbage, and, occasionally, the chicks of other birds

FOUND IN: A range of habitats, from icy regions of the Arctic to the deserts of North Africa

NEW CALEDONIAN CROW
(Corvus moneduloides)

There are no grub-eating woodpeckers on the islands of New Caledonia, so this intelligent crow has seized its opportunity. To extract grubs hiding in tree bark, the Caledonian crow carefully prepares special twigs and leaves, which it uses to poke and probe at the entrances of the grubs' burrows.

When a grub bites the stick, thinking it is a predator, the Caledonian crow gently pulls it out and eats the grub, still gripping onto the end.

LENGTH: 40–43 cm

DIET: Eggs and chicks, nuts, seeds, insects, spiders, and snails

FOUND IN: The forests of New Caledonia

CALIFORNIA SCRUB-JAY

(Aphelocoma californica)

The California scrub-jay has the finest memory of all birds. In the fall, it can stash away in different cracks and crevices more than 200 seeds and nuts, remembering the location of each one to come back to later.

Scrub-jays regularly steal the stores of other birds too, watching carefully where they bury them. If being watched, to fool its rivals, the California scrub-jay regularly finds and reburies its food elsewhere, safe from prying eyes.

LENGTH: 28–30 cm

DIET: Frogs, lizards, bird chicks, insects, nuts, and berries

FOUND IN: California's oak woodlands and evergreen forests and Australasia

EURASIAN NUTCRACKER

(Nucifraga caryocatactes)

With a beak like a jackhammer, the Eurasian nutcracker makes short work of most nuts and seeds. Its unique forked tongue, tipped with fingernail-like armor, means it can retrieve seeds from even the toughest pine cones.

Like other corvids, the Eurasian nutcracker regularly digs small burrows in which it buries its food. However, rarely does this species remember every single seed buried. The seeds that are forgotten grow into new trees, helping the forest to grow.

LENGTH: 32–35 cm

DIET: Seeds, nuts and animals, including small birds, eggs, and chicks

FOUND IN: Conifer forests across northern parts of Europe and Asia

FAIRYWRENS AND GRASSWRENS

Fairywrens and grasswrens, also known as Australian wrens, are small or medium-sized birds known for their striking songs. Though they are very wren-like, these charismatic birds are not closely related to wrens found in other parts of the world.

SUPERB FAIRYWREN
(*Malurus cyaneus*)

The superb fairywren is a master at picking up new songs. Even when still inside the egg, it can listen to songs outside and learn them for when it hatches. Unhatched chicks are particularly good at picking up the songs of their parents, especially the male, who sings most of all.

The superb fairywren can also tune into alarm calls made by other birds. By tapping into the high-pitched warning calls of other species, this enigmatic fairywren stays one step ahead of predators.

LENGTH: 15–20 cm

DIET: Insects, especially ants, grasshoppers, shield bugs, flies, and beetles

FOUND IN: Woodlands throughout southeast Australia

WALLACE'S FAIRYWREN
(*Sipodotus wallacii*)

This secretive fairywren is most often identified by the hissing calls that it gives off as it moves through the undergrowth. In small flocks, while hunting for food, individuals use these calls to keep in touch with one another, so that no-one strays too far from the group.

Like many small birds, Wallace's fairywren finds insects by probing its beak into cracks in tree bark and among tangled leaves and twigs. This gleaning behavior is especially helpful for finding insect grubs and caterpillars.

LENGTH: 11–12.5 cm

DIET: Insects and spiders

FOUND IN: Forests and some lowland plains of New Guinea

STRIATED GRASSWREN
(Amytornis striatus)

The small, rounded wings of the striated grasswren are not well-suited to long periods of sustained flight. This means that when disturbed by predators, the striated grasswren flees by hopping through the undergrowth, periodically flying before dropping to the forest floor like a bouncing ball.

The striated grasswren is especially common across Australia, hiding and nesting in the spiky, twisting grasses that grow in sandy places.

LENGTH: 14.5–19 cm

DIET: Beetles, ants, seeds, and other plants

FOUND IN: Sandy plains and dunes throughout southeastern Australia

DUSKY GRASSWREN
(Amytornis purnelli)

With its speckled wings and chest, the dusky grasswren is hard to spot as it hops between boulders in the deserts of central Australia. The species is most easily located by listening for its extraordinary range of different calls. These include metallic clinking sounds, high-pitched whistles, and twittering, along with flute-like warbling choruses.

The song of the dusky grasswren is different depending on where it lives. Southern dusky grasswrens sing slightly softer songs than their northern rivals, whose notes come out more sharply. Accents like these can be common in birds that sing.

LENGTH: 15.5–18 cm

DIET: Insects, spiders, seeds, and small desert fruits

FOUND IN: Rocky outcrops throughout central Australia

FINCHES

These perching birds are known for their cone-shaped beaks, often used for pulling apart seeds. Finches fly in a bouncing manner. Throughout human history, their rich and melodious songs have seen many species trapped and kept as cagebirds.

AFRICAN FIREFINCH
(Lagonosticta rubricata)

The nest of the African firefinch is built like a basket, with a soft inner layer of carefully trimmed flowers, often lined with soft feathers. Like all finches, most of their nest-making talents come from watching others build nests, particularly their parents, and practising with a variety of different materials.

When nesting, the African firefinch becomes very wary of its nemesis, the indigobird. These cuckoo-like brood parasites like to lay their own eggs in the African firefinch's nest to save themselves the energy of rearing chicks.

LENGTH: 10–11.5 cm

DIET: Seeds and, occasionally, insects

FOUND IN: Forest edges and river clearings across sub-Sarahan Africa

EURASIAN BULLFINCH
(Pyrrhula pyrrhula)

Unlike other finches, the Eurasian bullfinch has a special pouch on the floor of its mouth to help carry seeds back to the nest. Its stocky wings help it to travel far further than other finches in search of food.

The Eurasian bullfinch also eats the leaf buds of trees, just as they sprout in spring. A single bullfinch can eat up to thirty buds a minute. Many centuries ago, this habit saw Eurasian bullfinches treated with suspicion by fruit-growers.

LENGTH: 14.5–16 cm

FOUND IN: Woodlands across Europe and Asia

DIET: Seeds and leaf buds

AMERICAN GOLDFINCH
(Spinus tristis)

For a few weeks each spring, the American goldfinch develops a furious temper. Individuals peck at one another's feathers and attack with their legs and feet extended. These challenges help goldfinches, many of whom live close to one another, to work out who gets the best nesting places.

The American goldfinch nests later in the spring than any other North American finch. This is because it must waits early summer to breed, when there are enough seeds around to feed to its young.

LENGTH: 11–13 cm

FOUND IN: Fields, meadows, and floodplains across North America

DIET: Seeds and, occasionally, leaf buds and insects

'I'IWI
(Drepanis coccinea)

Pronounced "ee-EE-vee," this charming finch is one of the most common birds in Hawai'i. Its long beak is used to drink nectar from tube-like flowers that grow on shrubs and trees throughout its territory.

Hawai'i, like many islands, has been important in the evolution of new bird species. A single finch ancestor that made it to Hawai'i millions of years ago has since evolved into more than fifty new finch species, each adapted to its local conditions. Sadly, many have recently faced extinction.

LENGTH: 15 cm

FOUND IN: Forests of Hawai'i

DIET: Nectar and, occasionally, insects and spiders

GRASSHOPPER WARBLERS, GRASSBIRDS, AND BUSH WARBLERS

These perching songbirds form a group known as the Locustellidae. The name is a reference to their calls, which sound like noisy locusts or grasshoppers. These small birds feed on insects and mostly live in scrublands.

COMMON GRASSHOPPER WARBLER
(Locustella naevia)

The common grasshopper warbler can call for up to three minutes without pausing for breath. Its strange song comes out in pulses that rise and fall. Despite causing its whole body to vibrate, this rhythm ensures the call travels as far as it can.

Should a female come near, the male common grasshopper warbler does all it can to maintain her interest, running up and down branches with its tail feathers spread, fluttering its wings and picking up leaves and grass stems to emphasize its nest-making skills.

LENGTH: 12–12.5 cm

DIET: Flies, moths, beetles, and other insects

FOUND IN: Breeds in grasslands and scrublands throughout Europe and Asia

BRISTLED GRASSBIRD
(Schoenicola striatus)

To protect itself from twigs and thorns as it scampers through the undergrowth, the bristled grassbird has a row of small, stiff feathers in front of its eyes that can be erected like a protective visor. During the breeding season, males emerge from their hiding places to perform a charismatic, zig-zagging aerial dance before parachuting on open wings back into the scrub.

Once common across the Indian subcontinent, this species has been lost from much of its former range. This is likely to be because its grassland and marshland habitats are disappearing due to human actions.

LENGTH: 21 cm

DIET: Insects, particularly grasshoppers

FOUND IN: Grassy marshlands throughout the Indian subcontinent

NEW ZEALAND FERNBIRD

(Poodytes punctatus)

Like others in its group, the New Zealand fernbird is a reluctant flier. Rather than waste energy on flying, it prefers to hop from branch to branch and creep through undergrowth while searching for food.

Māori call the New Zealand fernbird the "wise bird." Its whistling, clicking calls were used to predict success or failure before fishing or hunting trips. Sometimes, they were thought to predict impending doom or disaster.

LENGTH: 18 cm

FOUND IN: Wetlands throughout New Zealand

DIET: Insects, including caterpillars, beetles, flies, and moths

SRI LANKA BUSH WARBLER

(Elaphrornis palliseri)

To find out which patches of forests this species lives in, scientists listen out for its explosive song—a loud "QUEEEEEET" call that rings out from dense scrub.

Like many warblers, the male and female Sri Lanka bush warbler look almost identical. Youngsters, on the other hand, lack the bright chest and underside that the adults possess. By looking different from the adults, young warblers show that they are not in competition to breed, meaning that fewer rivals may act aggressively toward them. This difference in color between adults and young is common across many bird species.

LENGTH: 15–16 cm

FOUND IN: Highland forests of Sri Lanka

DIET: Insects

GROUND BABBLERS

These secretive songbirds are found in tropical regions. Though they look like thrushes or warblers, ground babblers often have patches of feathers on the top of the head and on their eyebrows. Scientists can use these feather patterns to tell one species of ground babbler from another.

RUFOUS-WINGED FULVETTA
(Schoeniparus castaneceps)

This noisy ground babbler sings with a special "ti-du-di-du-di-du-di-du-di-du" song. Unusually, its wheezy calls can be heard throughout the day, even in the late afternoon when other birds go quiet. This makes the rufous-winged fulvetta easier to locate than other babblers.

Built by both the male and female, its nest is a carefully crafted dome made from moss, dry bamboo and plant roots that are stitched together with fine grasses and stalks. Hidden away upon tree trunks or hanging in creepers, these nests are very hard to spot.

LENGTH: 10–13 cm

DIET: Insects and, occasionally, tree sap

FOUND IN: Evergreen forests throughout Asia

PUFF-THROATED BABBLER
(Pellorneum ruficeps)

The puff-throated babbler is often mistaken for a mouse. This is because it scurries quickly in and out of its igloo-shaped nest that is made on the ground among the roots of dense bushes. To avoid predators, including snakes, its hatchlings grow quickly. Within two weeks, each chick is strong enough to leave the nest (fledge).

As adults, puff-throated babblers can be spotted in small groups on the forest floor. Here, they turn over leaves to catch tiny insects hiding underneath.

LENGTH: 15–17 cm

DIET: Insects

FOUND IN: Scrublands and bamboo forests across Asia, including the foothills of the Himalayan mountains

ABBOTT'S BABBLER
(Malacocincla abbotti)

To keep predators at bay, the Abbott's babbler nests high up in trees and surrounds itself with as many spiny thorns as possible. Here, it lays two batches of eggs during the breeding season, back to back, with no break. Sometimes the first batch of hatchlings are still in the nest, begging for food, when the second batch hatches.

When fully grown, the Abbott's babbler is wary of its nemesis, the violet cuckoo. This sly bird regularly seeks out the nest of this babbler, using it as free child-care for its young.

LENGTH: 15–17 cm

DIET: Insects

FOUND IN: Evergreen forests throughout South and Southeast Asia

FALCATED WREN-BABBLER
(Ptilocichla falcata)

The falcated wren-babbler gets its name from the falcon-like beak that it uses to tear apart large insects and scorpions. Its orange cap and white chin make it easy to tell apart from other babblers.

With fewer than 20,000 living in the wild, the falcated wren-babbler is one of many ground babblers threatened with extinction. It lives in just ten different patches of forest. Many of these patches are threatened by illegal logging, so scientists are working hard to protect more of its habitats.

LENGTH: 19–20 cm

DIET: Insects and scorpions

FOUND IN: Evergreen forests on the island of Palawan in the Philippines

PARROTS AND ALLIES | PERCHING BIRDS | PIGEONS AND DOVES | TUNNEL-NESTERS | WATERBIRDS | FORGOTTEN BIRDS

HONEYEATERS

These perching birds feed on nectar from flowers. Unlike hummingbirds, which hover from flower to flower, honeyeaters fly from perch to perch, leaning their long beaks into nearby flowers, sometimes hanging upside down as they do so. This large family contains 186 species, all found in Australasia.

NEW HOLLAND HONEYEATER
(Phylidonyris novaehollandiae)

Nectar isn't the only sugary liquid that the New Holland honeyeater likes to eat. It regularly raids trees where tiny aphid-like insects gather, to peck at the sugary liquid (known as honeydew) that the insects squirt out as waste. To gather enough protein to make its bright colors, the New Holland honeyeater also catches spiders and insects.

Without the New Holland honeyeater, Australia's shrubland habitats would look very different. This is because, when moving from flower to flower, honeyeaters move pollen around, helping forest plants reproduce.

LENGTH: 16–20 cm

FOUND IN: Shrublands across southern Australia

DIET: Nectar, honeydew, insects, and spiders

EASTERN SPINEBILL
(Acanthorhynchus tenuirostris)

When nectar supplies are low, the eastern spinebill changes its daily routine. Instead of resting, it dedicates more of its day to finding new flowers and feeds for longer, converting much of the sugar in its diet to fat, which it stores for later.

The eastern spinebill can also lower the speed at which its stomach breaks down food, making each meal last for longer. These energy-saving adaptations have led to the eastern spinebill spreading into many new habitats across Australia, including parks and gardens.

LENGTH: 13–16 cm

FOUND IN: Dry forests and scrublands in southeastern Australia

DIET: Nectar, insects, and spiders

MACGREGOR'S HONEYEATER
(Macgregoria pulchra)

The MacGregor's honeyeater times its mating season around the ripening of seeds on a special kind of conifer tree that is found only in remote parts of the forest. The conifer's high-energy seeds give this honeyeater many of the chemicals it needs to grow its eye-catching orange feathers, which are used to attract mates.

Though its colors make it easy to spot, the nesting habits of the MacGregor's honeyeater remain mysterious. Though this honeyeater was discovered more than a century ago, only three nests have so far been studied in detail by scientists.

LENGTH: 35–40 cm

DIET: Fruits and, less commonly, insects and nectar

FOUND IN: Isolated woodlands and forests across New Guinea

NEW ZEALAND BELLBIRD
(Anthornis melanura)

This honeyeater gets its name for its curious song, which explorer Captain Cook noted, many centuries ago, was "like small bells most exquisitely tuned." The tinkly song is often heard in the early morning or in the late evening.

Like all honeyeaters, the New Zealand bellbird has a brush-like tongue that it uses to sip at nectar and scrape honeydew from plants, especially beech trees. While feeding, its face often becomes covered in flower pollen from lots of different plants. When it moves from tree to tree, this pollen is spread to new flowers, helping the forest grow.

LENGTH: 17–20 cm

DIET: Nectar, fruits, and honeydew

FOUND IN: Dense forests of New Zealand

LARKS

Larks are known for their long and complicated songs, which are often performed from high in the sky during the breeding season. Though many species look alike, there are small differences in their habitats and daily behaviors. In total, 100 types of lark have been discovered. Most live in Europe, Africa, and Asia.

EURASIAN SKYLARK
(Alauda arvensis)

The male skylark's song, delivered while hovering up to 100 meters in the sky, is a test of endurance. The female skylark uses the length of the skylark's song to assess how healthy the male is. The longer the song, the more desirable the mate. During the breeding season, a single Eurasian skylark song can last twenty minutes or more.

The nest of the Eurasian skylark is a shallow scratch in the ground lined with grasses, hidden among thick vegetation, including farmland crops.

LENGTH: 17–19 cm

DIET: Insects, seeds, and young leaves

FOUND IN: Grasslands and farmlands across Europe, Asia and north Africa

GREATER HOOPOE-LARK
(Alaemon alaudipes)

To stay alive in its desert habitats, the greater hoopoe-lark adjusts the levels of fat in its skin to stop water from escaping the body. This adaptation is so effective that the greater hoopoe-lark can survive for weeks without drinking any liquid at all. All the water it needs is absorbed from the food it eats.

When the rainy season arrives, the greater hoopoe-lark develops an appetite for snails. It smashes their shells by dropping them from a great height onto rocks.

LENGTH: 19–23 cm

DIET: Mostly insects, along with small reptiles, amphibians, and snails

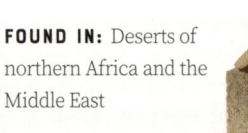

FOUND IN: Deserts of northern Africa and the Middle East

SAND LARK
(Alaudala raytal)

As well as singing a long, complicated song while hovering, the sand lark also produces a second song, which features a series of rattling, whistling notes, when nearer the ground. By regularly pausing during hovering and opening its wings, the sand lark softly parachutes downward, attracting the attention of nearby females.

Like many larks, the sand lark frequently adds the calls of other birds into its songs. It regularly mimics the calls of lapwings and sparrows.

LENGTH: 10–13 cm

DIET: Insects and seeds

FOUND IN: Dry, sandy rivers and lakes from Iran to Pakistan

RUFOUS-NAPED LARK
(Mirafra africana)

Termite mounds, bushes, and fence posts are just some of the perches that the rufous-naped lark sings from. After performing its song twenty times in a row, this lark vibrates its wings, shaking them so fast that they make an eerie, rattling sound.

Found across more than 4 million square miles of Africa, the rufous-naped lark is a very adaptable lark. Its success is partly down to its fondness for grassy habitats kept short by cattle as they feed. Grasslands like these have become common in many regions of Africa, helping the rufous-naped lark spread.

LENGTH: 15–20 cm

DIET: Insects, spiders, millipedes, and worms

FOUND IN: Bushy grasslands and savannas throughout sub-Saharan Africa

LAUGHINGTHRUSHES AND ALLIES

Known for their chuckling calls, this group of noisy perching birds contains more than 130 species. Most laughingthrushes eat insects, hunting them while hopping through the undergrowth or gleaning them from leaves. Many species live in South and Southeast Asia.

WHITE-CRESTED LAUGHINGTHRUSH
(Garrulax leucolophus)

The white-crested laughingthrush has a black "mask" around the eyes. This feather pattern, which many birds possess, reduces glare from the sun and helps the laughingthrush keep track of its prey when the sun is low.

When small flocks of white-crested laughingthrushes move through the undergrowth, they give off lots of calls to stay in contact with one another, including grunts, chirps and, when startled by a predator, loud cackles. These cackling calls inspire laughingthrushes in the flock to rally together and surround the predator, guiding it away from their territory. This behavior is known as mobbing.

LENGTH: 26–31 cm

FOUND IN: Foothill forests of South and Southeast Asia

DIET: Insects and spiders, along with nectar, fruits, and seeds

JUNGLE BABBLER
(Argya striata)

The jungle babbler's nickname is "seven sisters," so called for its habit of moving together through the undergrowth in noisy social groups that often contain seven individuals. These groups regularly gather to preen one another's feathers before sleep. This behavior helps keep relationships between individuals extra-strong.

Unusually among birds, jungle babblers also play with one another, engaging in rough-and-tumble games. Playing may help young babblers work out who the toughest birds in the pack are, and which birds it is best to avoid later in life.

LENGTH: 25 cm

FOUND IN: Forests and gardens throughout South Asia

DIET: Insects, as well as grains, nectar, and berries

ARROW-MARKED BABBLER
(Turdoides jardineii)

Like many laughingthrushes, nest-building by the arrow-marked babbler is a family affair. Up to eight individuals in the group work together to build a bowl-shaped nest from grasses, reeds, decaying leaves, and dried flower stems. The nest is hidden in the forest canopy, among creepers and tangled branches.

When the eggs of the arrow-marked babbler are laid, every individual in the family takes it in turns to watch over them. This teamwork approach to nesting helps the arrow-marked babbler protect itself from pesky cuckoos looking for a place to secretly lay their own eggs.

LENGTH: 22–25 cm

FOUND IN: Woodlands of tropical Africa

DIET: Termites, crickets, grasshoppers, and other insects, along with seeds and fruits

HIMALAYAN CUTIA
(Cutia nipalensis)

Living in mountain forests, the Himalayan cutia creeps nimbly across tree trunks and branches, scouring cracks and crevices with its beak to find insects and snails. Every now and then, scientists have observed the Himalayan cutia eating tiny stones and pebbles, known as grit. When swallowed, grit helps mash up food in the stomach, helping birds extract more energy from their meals.

Because the Himalayan cutia lives in such a remote part of the world, very little is known about its mating or nesting behaviors. In future, new research expeditions will help scientists discover more.

LENGTH: 17–19 cm

FOUND IN: Broadleaf evergreen forests in the foothills of the Himalayas

DIET: Insects, snails, seeds, and berries

LEAF WARBLERS

These small, very nervous, birds rarely rest. For most of the day, leaf warblers move through branches and twigs, often flicking their wings urgently as they search for insects. Compared to other perching birds, leaf-warbler songs are simple, sometimes consisting of just one or two notes.

PALLAS'S LEAF WARBLER
(Phylloscopus proregulus)

As light as a sheet of paper, Pallas's leaf warbler is one of the smallest perching birds in the world. Its small size allows it to hover in front of insects or, less commonly, dangle off twigs and branches to investigate cracks and crannies where insects like to hide.

In conifer woodlands, Pallas's leaf warbler can be very common indeed, with up to fifty pairs nesting in every square kilometer of forest. Its nests, carefully arranged at the base of tree branches, are made of twigs and leaves, bound together with hair, feathers, and fine grasses.

LENGTH: 9–10 cm

DIET: Insects and spiders

FOUND IN: Breeds in conifer woodlands across Siberia and surrounding regions

LIMESTONE LEAF WARBLER
(Phylloscopus calciatilis)

This secretive leaf warbler was first seen by scientists more than thirty years ago, while exploring the limestone forests of Vietnam and Laos. For years, scientists thought it was just like any other leaf warbler, but years later, they noticed that the limestone leaf warbler was smaller and more stripy than others living nearby. In 2009, it was declared as a new species.

In biology, the rule is that the discoverer of a new species is allowed the honor of naming it. The scientists that discovered the limestone leaf warbler used the Latin word *calciatilis*, which means "dwelling on limestone."

LENGTH: 10–11 cm

DIET: Unknown

FOUND IN: Forests in upland regions of Vietnam, Laos, and southern China

COMMON CHIFFCHAFF
(Phylloscopus collybita)

The common chiffchaff is a small bird with a big temper. Crows, jays, magpies, and stoats are just some of the animals this warbler attempts to scare off during the breeding season, along with any love-rivals seeking to steal territory for themselves.

To maintain this high level of activity, the chiffchaff requires a rich diet of insects, particularly flies and caterpillars. During the nesting season, this leaf warbler needs to eat a third of its body weight in insects each day to survive. In the fall, to stock up its energy reserves before migrating 3,000 miles south to Africa, it adds sugar-rich berries and fruits to its diet.

The name chiffchaff comes from the sound of its call, which is an easy-to-recognize, high-pitched "CHIFF-CHAFF-CHIFF-CHAFF," sung high from the treetops. For this reason, in German, the chiffchaff is known as a *zilp-zalp* and in Welsh it is a *siff-saff*.

LENGTH: 11–12 cm

DIET: Insects, seeds, and berries

FOUND IN: Breeds in open woodlands across Europe and Asia

LONG-TAILED TITS

A small group of very active perching birds, long-tailed tits are known for their short beaks and long tails. They regularly form large flocks, numbering fifty or more, which move busily from tree to tree looking for insects. These flocks are kept together using a series of simple, trilling contact calls that are made by all members of the group.

LONG-TAILED BUSHTIT
(Aegithalos caudatus)

6,000 or more ingredients go into building the spectacular nest of the long-tailed bushtit. These items include spider silk, moss, and even tiny bits of shredded paper. Feathers, used to line the inside of the nest, are highly sought after. Long-tailed bushtit's also seek bright-green mossy lichens, which are used to make a camouflaged coating on the surface of the nest to hide it from predators.

In winter, to reduce the chances of freezing, long-tailed bushtits often roost communally, squashing together at night in birdboxes and other tight spaces to try to keep warm.

LENGTH: 13–16 cm

DIET: Insects, especially caterpillars of moths and butterflies

FOUND IN: Woodlands, scrublands, and heathlands across Europe and Asia

PYGMY TIT
(Aegithalos exilis)

Able to rest comfortably in the palm of a human hand, the pygmy tit is one of the tiniest of all long-tailed tits. Its small size means it can search for insects, such as aphids and tiny spiders, that larger long-tailed tits overlook.

Like other long-tailed tits, the pygmy tit is very noisy when moving from tree to tree. Its metallic chirping is so high-pitched it can barely be heard by human ears. From a distance, it sounds like radio static.

LENGTH: 8–9 cm

DIET: Small insects

FOUND IN: Mountain forests and plantations on the island of Java

LYREBIRDS

With their eye-catching feathers, these ground-dwelling Australian birds look like birds of paradise. Their name comes from their S-shaped tail feathers, which look like a musical instrument called a lyre. Their songs, which often mimic the calls of other birds, are among the most complicated of all birds.

SUPERB LYREBIRD
(Menura novaehollandiae)

Able to copy the call of almost any bird, the superb lyrebird is the most gifted mimic of all. Up to eighty per cent of its songs include notes and calls heard from other birds that share its habitat. These calls, which young lyrebirds learn and practise in their early years, are often copied from adult lyrebirds.

When kept in captivity, lyrebirds regularly learn to mimic human words, mobile phone ringtones, and human machinery, such as cars and diggers. They have even been known to copy the sounds of dogs barking and babies crying.

LENGTH: 76–103 cm

FOUND IN: Forests of southeastern Australia

DIET: Insects, earthworms, and fungus

ALBERT'S LYREBIRD
(Menura alberti)

By raking aside leaves with its claws, the Albert's lyrebird makes a stage from which it performs to others nearby. Upon this stage, the male raises its tail feathers in the air, arches them over its head, and then begins to shake the rear half of its body, causing the reflective edges of each tail feather to vibrate hypnotically.

If impressed with this display, the female Albert's lyrebird lays a single egg in a nest of twigs held together with bark, ferns, and palm leaves. This carefully engineered nest can take almost three weeks to build.

LENGTH: 86–93 cm

FOUND IN: Isolated rainforests in eastern Australia

DIET: Insects and worms

MANAKINS

Manakins can make a host of charismatic calls using a unique voice box that differs slightly in shape and size between species. Whistles, trills, and buzzing noises are just some of the calling sounds produced by this group. These colorful birds, often with long, plume-like tail feathers, are found in tropical regions of the Americas.

ARARIPE MANAKIN
(Antilophia bokermanni)

The Araripe manakin is one of the rarest of all birds. It was discovered less than thirty years ago by scientists in northeastern Brazil on a fieldtrip in the rainforest. Once seen for the first time, scientists realized immediately that this was a very rare bird indeed, one that required immediate help to stop it from disappearing forever.

Today, studies show that as few as 1,000 Araripe manakins may survive in the wild. They are found in only a few patches of rainforest, only some of which are protected from logging. Right now, scientists are working hard to safeguard more of the Araripe manakin's precious habitats so that its future can be secured.

The dazzling head crown seen in the male Araripe manakin is related to its diet. The more beetles that the male eats, the healthier the male becomes and the redder its crown becomes. Females are especially interested in mating with healthy males, so they use the head crown as a way of finding the perfect mates to nest with. Unlike the male, the female Araripe manakin is very camouflaged and is far harder to spot.

LENGTH: 14–16 cm

DIET: Small fruits and insects

FOUND IN: Isolated rainforests in northeastern Brazil

STRIOLATED MANAKIN
(Machaeropterus striolatus)

With a churring, buzzing call, the song of the striolated manakin sounds more insect than bird. Yet, as with many birds, its songs have regional accents. In Venezuela, parts of the striolated manakin's song are sharper; in Colombia, its notes are higher pitched; and in Brazil, the song is gentler.

To help its calls travel as far as possible, males of this manakin species come together and sing in a chorus that can be heard by females in the surrounding territory.

LENGTH: 9–11 cm

FOUND IN: Western parts of the Amazon rainforest

DIET: Small fruits and insects

LONG-TAILED MANAKIN
(Chiroxiphia linearis)

The long-tailed manakin is the only bird in the world to make true friends for life. Pairs of males regularly buddy up together to build special courtship stages from which they sing a duet to attract females. Together, the two males repeat their song up to 5,000 times each day.

When a female investigates, males stop singing and begin to dance instead. This begins with the "popcorn dance," where the males take it in terns to jump and hover, and ends with a cartwheel-like routine where the two birds bounce over one another again and again.

LENGTH: 20–25 cm

FOUND IN: Forests across Central America

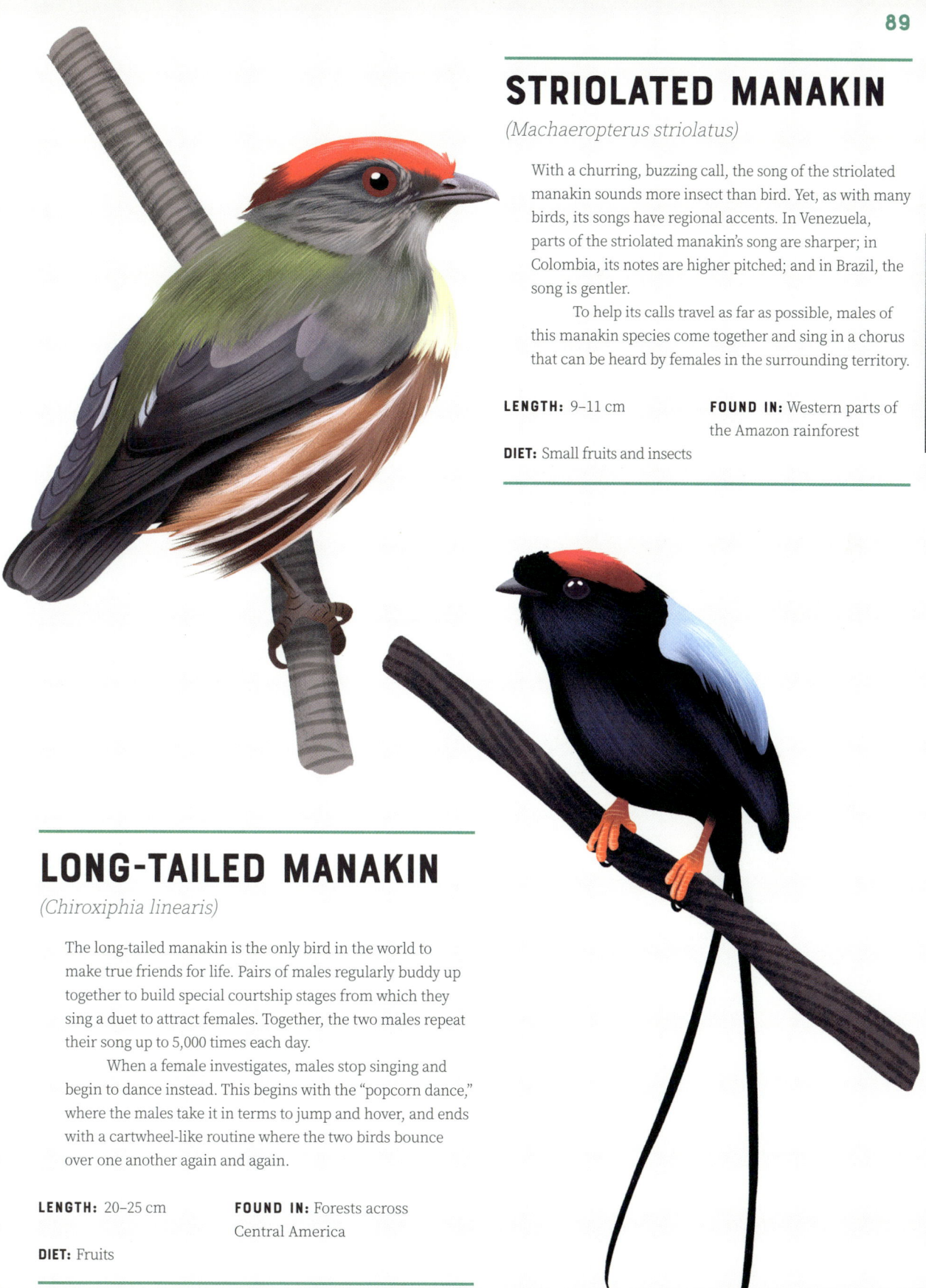

DIET: Fruits

AMERICAN BLACKBIRDS

These adaptable birds live across the American continents. Though they look alike, American blackbirds are not closely related to the blackbirds of Europe, Asia, and Africa. Over 100 species are known, living in a range of habitats including grasslands, swamps, and forests.

BOBOLINK
(Dolichonyx oryzivorus)

The bobolink is a friend to farmers. Every year, these blackbirds eat thousands of moths, stopping them from laying eggs that hatch into hungry caterpillars that destroy crops. Sadly, due to habitat loss, the number of bobolinks is decreasing. In some areas, compared to forty years ago, just a quarter of the total number of bobolink remain.

No-one knows the true reason for the name bobolink. It may have been a shortening of Robert of Lincoln, a historic English bishop whose name, some argue, can be heard among the rich, flute-like notes that this bird makes in spring.

LENGTH: 15–21 cm

DIET: Insects and seeds

FOUND IN: Breeds in grasslands across North America

WESTERN MEADOWLARK
(Sturnella neglecta)

Named for its melodic, lark-like song, this American blackbird is one of the most widespread birds in the world. It finds food by pushing its beak into the ground and then opening it as wide as it can, splitting apart clumps of soils where seeds or insects may be hiding. This strategy, used by many blackbirds, is called gaping.

The western meadowlark's stomach works very quickly. A meal takes just four hours to be fully digested, and so the stomach needs to be regularly filled up. In a single day, this meadowlark can fill its stomach three times over.

LENGTH: 19–21 cm

DIET: Seeds and insects

FOUND IN: Nests in open grasslands across North America

AMERICAN CARDINALS

Known for their fiery red, dazzling yellow, and bright-blue plumages, the cardinals are eye-catching birds that live in the Americas. Fifty-three species are known, most living in the treetops. These birds lay eggs in open-top nests that are cared for by both males and females.

PAINTED BUNTING
(Passerina ciris)

With its dash of rainbow-like colors, the male painted bunting bows and quivers its wings while fluffing up its feathers to look as noticeable as a possible. As well as being eye-catching to females, these colorful displays can attract the attention of rival male birds, causing violent scuffles and, sometimes, death.

Like many birds, the painted bunting sheds (molts) its feathers after the breeding season and then grows new ones. During the molting period, birds are especially vulnerable to predators.

LENGTH: 12–13 cm

DIET: Seeds, especially grass seeds

FOUND IN: Breeds in scrublands and gardens across southern USA and northern Mexico

RED-CROWNED ANT-TANAGER
(Habia rubica)

Poised and ready to strike, the red-crowned ant-tanager pays close attention to swarms of army ants as they move across the forest floor. As the ant colony invades new territory, insects and spiders try to get out of their way, only to fall prey to the sharp eyes of this hungry insect predator lying in wait.

The red-crowned ant-tanager was once thought to be part of the bird group known as tanagers, hence the common name. Scientists now think this bird should be part of the American cardinals. The science of grouping animals (known as taxonomy) is a complicated job for bird scientists.

LENGTH: 17–19 cm

DIET: Insects and berries

FOUND IN: Forests across many parts of Central and South America

AMERICAN SPARROWS

These American perching birds look like the sparrows of Africa, Asia, and Europe. They use their cone-shaped beaks to remove the hard shells of seeds before eating them. Unlike most sparrows, which are often camouflaged and hard to spot, some tropical American sparrows have colorful, eye-catching feather patterns.

WHITE-CROWNED SPARROW
(Zonotrichia leucophrys)

To save time on its fourteen-day migration, the white-crowned sparrow sleeps while flying. To manage this, half of its brain switches off, while the other side remains alert. Every few hours, the active and sleeping parts of the brain swap. This keeps the brain rested, allowing the white-crowned sparrow to arrive at its North American breeding grounds in the best shape possible.

Partly because of this adaptation, within seven days of the white-crowned sparrow's arrival, it has set up its territory and is already defending it from rival males, using its charismatic, whistling song.

LENGTH: 15–16 cm

DIET: Seeds and insects

FOUND IN: Breeds in mountainous snow forests and tundra in remote North America

SONG SPARROW
(Melospiza melodia)

The song sparrow takes in the songs of nearby sparrows, learns the best bits, and then memorizes and repeats a thirty-minute "playlist" that it performs each morning. It makes sure to shuffle its songs for females, so that its full repertoire can be heard.

These songs can often be heard in gardens, where they can sometimes attract the interest of hungry cats. Experiments suggest that song sparrows learn to avoid cats by watching how other birds react to them.

LENGTH: 12–17 cm

DIET: Seeds, fruits, and insects

FOUND IN: Forests and shrublands, often near wetlands, throughout North America

AMERICAN WARBLERS

These small and often colorful perching birds are found only in the Americas. The group includes 117 species, and although the name suggests that they sing flute-like "warbling" songs, many species produce more complicated songs that include hissing, buzzing, and clucking sounds.

OVENBIRD
(Seiurus aurocapilla)

This American warbler is named for its strange nest, which, when arranged on the ground, looks like an old-fashioned oven. The domed structure, held together with grasses and leaves, has a side entrance through which the male and female enter with food for their chicks.

The ovenbird's ground-nests are often raided by predators, especially chipmunks. To prepare for intruders, the adult ovenbird has learned to eavesdrop on chipmunk calls and can use them to judge how close these predators may be.

LENGTH: 15 cm

DIET: Ants, beetles, and seeds

FOUND IN: Dense forests of southern Canada and central USA

PROTHONOTARY WARBLER
(Protonotaria citrea)

In spring, the prothonotary warbler desperately scurries up and down tree trunks looking for holes of just the right size to build a nest in. Once the nest is built, male and female warblers violently defend it from their rivals, sometimes locking beaks and feet in midair and tumbling to the ground in combat.

This American warbler is one of many garden birds to have benefited from people putting up wooden birdboxes. Birdboxes save the prothonotary warbler lots of time and effort finding a suitable tree trunk in which to nest.

LENGTH: 14 cm

DIET: Insects, spiders, and crustaceans, as well as fruits and seeds

FOUND IN: Breeds near swamps across North America

AFROEURASIAN FLYCATCHERS

More than 350 types of these nimble perching birds are known. As the name suggests, most species are especially fond of eating flies, which they track through the air with large, sensitive eyes. Afroeurasian flycatchers live in forests throughout Europe, Asia, and Africa.

EUROPEAN ROBIN
(Erithacus rubecula)

The European robin often follows wild pigs through the undergrowth. When these large animals disturb insects or worms hiding in the soil, the robin nips in and scoops up its meal. Robins regularly approach human gardeners for the same reason, particularly when they are digging.

The European robin is a fierce defender of its territory and individuals regularly suffer injury from fights with their neighbors. Occasionally, in spring, males become so full of rage that they have even been known to attack their own reflection in a window.

LENGTH: 14 cm

DIET: Insects and spiders, as well as berries in winter

FOUND IN: Forests, grasslands, and gardens throughout Europe, Asia, and the northern tip of Africa

BLUETHROAT
(Luscinia svecica)

When displaying to a female, the male bluethroat shows off its blue plumage by pointing its beak to the sky and drooping its wings downward. If disturbed by another male during its performance, the male chases its rival away, sometimes flying more than 500 meters in angry pursuit.

During the breeding season, male bluethroats engage in singing "duels" with each other. The male with the strongest voice wins the territory dispute. Singing, rather than fighting, one another, means that individuals are less likely to end up injured during the breeding season.

LENGTH: 13–15 cm

DIET: Insects, as well as seeds and berries

FOUND IN: Shrublands and marshlands throughout Europe, Asia, and Alaska

EUROPEAN PIED FLYCATCHER
(Ficedula hypoleuca)

Flies are just a small part of the European pied flycatcher's diet. Ants make up a quarter of its meals, along with bees, wasps, and beetles. It has even been known to grab snails by the head and smash their hard shells against concrete.

While sitting on eggs, the female European pied flycatcher waits for the male to return with food to eat. Known as courtship feeding, this behavior helps strengthen the pair-bond between male and female before the eggs hatch. Some males tend to more than one female during this period, and so they often suffer from exhaustion.

LENGTH: 13 cm

DIET: Mostly insects

FOUND IN: Forests and gardens across Europe, Asia, and northern Africa

DESERT WHEATEAR
(Oenanthe deserti)

The desert wheatear weaves its nest in cracks or crevices found in its environment. Potential places for nests include collapsed walls, riverside banks, or, occasionally, the empty burrows of rats and mice. To keep its nest insulated, the desert wheatear lines it with fine grasses, wool or feathers.

Occasionally, the desert wheatear steals dead insects and spiders from ants as they carry them back to their nests. This thievery, known as kleptoparasitism, is rare in flycatchers.

LENGTH: 14–15 cm

DIET: Insects, woodlice, millipedes, and spiders

FOUND IN: Dry deserts and grasslands throughout the Middle East and Asia

AFROEURASIAN SPARROWS

Sparrows are small and plump birds with stocky beaks that help them break apart seeds. Many sparrows live in noisy colonies, especially on the sides of buildings. In some parts of the world, wily sparrows have become scavengers of human waste.

HOUSE SPARROW
(Passer domesticus)

Named for its love of human buildings, the house sparrow is one of the most social of all birds. A single roosting spot can be home to more than 10,000 sparrows, which all chatter loudly to one another. With so many eyes on the lookout for predators, colony-living helps keep sparrows safe.

With its adaptable nature, the house sparrow has spread across the world in recent centuries, both naturally and through accidental releases into the wild. It is now one of the world's most numerous and widespread birds.

LENGTH: 15–17 cm

FOUND IN: Towns and cities throughout the world

DIET: Seeds and insects

CAPE SPARROW
(Passer melanurus)

Unlike other birds, the Cape sparrow can make a variety of nests. Nests can be made of grasses and stuffed into cracks; they can be dome-shaped and hung in trees; or made of twigs and feathers and placed in the open. Sometimes the Cape sparrow uses nests that have been abandoned by other birds, such as swallows. Cape sparrows have even been known to nest in hay bales.

Sometimes, like cuckoos, Cape sparrows sneak their eggs into nests that are not their own. This behavior, known as brood parasitism, means that adults can produce young without the expense of having to feed them.

LENGTH: 14–16 cm

FOUND IN: Dry savannas across southern Africa

DIET: Seeds, leaf buds, and soft fruits

CHESTNUT SPARROW
(Passer eminibey)

Barely longer than a popsicle-stick, the chestnut sparrow is a small sparrow with a big attitude. This species regularly harasses other birds while they are constructing their own nests, sometimes spending many hours annoying them.

By bullying other birds while they are making a nest, the chestnut sparrow can sometimes force them, eventually, to give up and go elsewhere. At this point, the chestnut sparrow takes ownership of the half-finished nest, using it rent-free as a temporary home for its eggs.

LENGTH: 10–12 cm

DIET: Grass seeds, small beetles, and scraps of human food

FOUND IN: Dry savannas, fields, and villages across East Africa

RUSSET SPARROW
(Passer cinnamomeus)

The russet sparrow is the most musical of all sparrows. Far more than a classic sparrow "chirrup," its song is a lengthy "cheep chirrup cheeweep," interspersed with "chit-chit-chit" sounds that become more rapid when rival males are around.

Pairs of russet sparrows have been known to build their untidy treetop nests very close to black kite nests. This protects sparrow nestlings from predators, such as rats, who are wary of coming too close to hungry birds of prey.

LENGTH: 14–15 cm

DIET: Mostly seeds

FOUND IN: Grasslands and forests throughout eastern Asia and the Himalayas

OVENBIRDS

Ovenbirds get their name from the curious clay nests that some species build, which resemble an old-fashioned oven. In total, 315 types of ovenbird are known across many habitats. These include jungles, grasslands, coastal cliffs, and gardens. Most ovenbirds are especially fond of eating insects.

BROWN-BILLED SCYTHEBILL
(Campylorhamphus pusillus)

With a long, curved beak, the brown-billed scythebill probes the gaps in bark, mosses, and tangled vines, looking for beetles. This bird avoids the lower branches of trees, favoring the mossy upper branches where it can remain as hidden as possible. It can scurry on the tops of branches, but also, regularly, hunts upside down on the underside of the canopy.

Being very hard to spot, little is known about the courtship behavior of the brown-billed scythebill. Some scientists think this ovenbird may pair for life, while others think it pairs only for a season or two.

LENGTH: 20–25 cm

DIET: Insects, especially beetles

FOUND IN: Rainforests of Colombia, Costa Rica, Ecuador, Panama, Peru, and Venezuela

SLENDER-BILLED MINER
(Geositta tenuirostris)

With sharp eyes and a long beak, the slender-billed miner works the soil looking for beetles, grubs, and spiders. It has even been known to feed on tiny soil animals known as springtails, that are barely the size of a full stop on this page.

The slender-billed miner doesn't build an oven-nest like others in its family. Instead, its grass-filled nests are placed in tunnels dug into the ground, hence the name "miner." These tunnels are occasionally lined with cattle hair to help insulate the eggs.

LENGTH: 16–18 cm

DIET: Insects and spiders

FOUND IN: Grasslands and farmlands in Argentina, Bolivia, Ecuador, and Peru

OLIVACEOUS WOODCREEPER
(Sittasomus griseicapillus)

Few insects are safe from the hungry olivaceous woodcreeper. This elusive ovenbird has been spotted chasing swarms of army ants, attacking flying termites, and tracking monkeys through the canopy, picking off the insects disturbed by their movement. As with other ovenbirds, beetles are an important part of its diet.

For much of the year, the olivaceous woodcreeper moves in flocks through the forest. During the breeding season, it seeks out unused burrows in trees made by woodpeckers. Hidden from view in tree holes and crevices, almost nothing is known about its eggs or chicks.

LENGTH: 13–19 cm

DIET: Mostly insects

FOUND IN: Rainforests and scrublands across South America

WING-BANDED HORNERO
(Furnarius figulus)

Often working in pairs, the wing-banded hornero walks over the ground, picking up leaves and stones to uncover beetles and spiders lurking beneath. Unlike other ovenbirds, which mostly eat insects, the wing-banded hornero also eats snails.

To keep its eggs safe from watchful predators, pairs of wing-banded horneros hide them in nests at the top of palm trees, where the thick branches meet. Here, the chunky, interwoven leaf stems act like protective bars on a cage. Within twenty days of hatching, the chicks are ready to fledge.

LENGTH: 15–16 cm

DIET: Mostly insects

FOUND IN: Woodlands, marshlands, and gardens throughout Brazil

PIPITS AND WAGTAILS

While walking, these birds bob their tails up and down rhythmically, hence the name "wagtail." Found mostly in Africa, Europe, and Asia, these keen-eyed perching birds spend a surprising amount of their lives on the ground, where they search for insects, worms, and spiders. Often, these birds make nests on the ground, containing up to six speckled eggs.

WHITE WAGTAIL
(Motacilla alba)

No-one knows for sure why the white wagtail walks with such an exaggerated bobbing tail. Some scientists think the movement helps flush insects from the grass, while others argue it is a friendly signal to put rival wagtails at ease or that it makes nearby predators think the wagtail knows they are there.

The white wagtail is celebrated for the unusual places it sometimes lays its eggs. Nests have been found in beaver dams, within the nests of golden eagles, and, once, in the skull of a dead walrus.

LENGTH: 16–18 cm

DIET: Worms, spiders, and insects, especially flies

FOUND IN: Numerous habitats across most of Europe and Asia

PADDYFIELD PIPIT
(Anthus rufulus)

When young mosquitos hatch from water in great swarms, the paddyfield pipit becomes very excited. It dashes and swoops into the air, snatching insects while flying, before returning to the floor to momentarily rest.

When back at its nest in the ground, the paddyfield pipit vomits half-digested insects into the mouths of its chicks. Should a predator approach the nest after seeing the parent bird enter with food, the adult pipit runs from the nest, pretending it has a broken wing. This tricks the predator into attacking the adult and not the chicks.

LENGTH: 15–16 cm

DIET: Insects, including beetles, mosquitos, and flying termites

FOUND IN: Open grasslands throughout southern Asia

WATER PIPIT
(Anthus spinoletta)

When ready to nest, the female water pipit watches the courtship flights of males in its neighborhood. During these displays, the male water pipit climbs up to 30 meters, before looping downward in an arc, singing a simple song that contains six repetitions of a different short note.

In some parts of Europe and Asia, the female water pipit gets a ravenous hunger for snails during the breeding season. This is because snail shells are rich in calcium, which female birds need to make their eggshells. Without enough calcium, bird eggs become soft and crack too easily.

LENGTH: 15–17 cm

DIET: Insects, snails, spiders, woodlice, and millipedes

FOUND IN: Mountain meadows throughout southern Europe and Asia

MADANGA
(Anthus ruficollis)

The madanga, a close relative of the pipits, lives on a single Indonesian island known as Buru. Unlike other pipits and wagtails, this species rarely hunts on the ground. Instead, it runs its beak through gaps in tree trunks, feeling for insects hidden from view.

Because its forest habitats are threatened by logging and other human activities, scientists have listed the madanga as an endangered species. Very little is known of the behavior of this bird and nothing is known of its song, which no scientist has yet recorded.

LENGTH: 13 cm

DIET: Insects

FOUND IN: Mountain forests of Buru, Indonesia

PITTAS

Pittas are a family of short, stout perching birds that are mostly found in Southeast Asia. Compared to other perching birds, pittas spend lots of time on their own, skulking on forest floors looking for worms and insects to eat. Males and females build a large, domed nest hidden in trees and bushes.

MALAYAN BANDED PITTA
(Hydrornis irena)

The Malayan banded pitta is very choosy about where it constructs its large nest, which can be bigger than a bowling ball. Made with grasses and dry, crushed-up leaves, the nest is often placed 2 or 3 meters above ground, sometimes in the thorniest bushes the adult can find. Thorns act as a natural barrier to predators, including rats and snakes.

Malayan banded pitta hatchlings are fed a diet of earthworms, collected by the parent birds. Like chickens, this pitta uses its feet to scratch at the floor to expose small animals hiding under soil.

LENGTH: 20–23 cm

DIET: Worms, insect grubs, and snails

FOUND IN: Lowland forests of Thailand, Malaysia, and Sumatra

WESTERN HOODED PITTA
(Pitta sordida)

At some times of year, when winged termites start to swarm from their nests, the western hooded pitta stands ready. Leaping into the air, it takes insects as they fly past, consuming as many as possible. Some scientists think this bird can eat its own body weight in insects each day.

In some habitats, it is likely that the western hooded pitta travels across water between islands and mainland Asia. Individuals mostly fly at night, guided by the moon's light. Traveling at night keeps this pitta safe from day-flying hawks and eagles.

LENGTH: 16–19 cm

DIET: Insects, spiders, and snails

FOUND IN: Forests in eastern and southeastern Asia and on scattered Southeast Asian islands

FAIRY PITTA
(Pitta nympha)

Small and nymph-like, the fairy pitta is one of the smallest pittas. It nests in crevices between rocks a few meters above ground and lines its nest with mosses and lichens. Because of its small stature, staying warm is hard for the fairy pitta. The female fairy pitta cuddles up to its hatchlings for at least four days, depending totally on the male to find earthworms.

The cold is one reason why six out of ten hatchlings in each fairy pitta nest will fail to survive. Other threats to pitta hatchlings include chick-eating snakes, cats, monkeys, and crows.

LENGTH: 16–20 cm

FOUND IN: Breeds in the forests of East Asia

DIET: Worms, spiders, insects, and snails

NOISY PITTA
(Pitta versicolor)

The noisy pitta lives up to its name. Its loud song, a series of three notes that are each more high-pitched than the last, rings out first thing in the morning and last thing in the evening. It has even been known, during the breeding season, to continue singing through the night.

The word *pitta* means "quail" in a local Indian language. Pittas regularly delight birdwatchers. Some tourists make special trips to see as many pitta species as they can.

LENGTH: 19–21 cm

FOUND IN: Forests across eastern Australia and southern New Guinea

DIET: Worms, insects, and snails

REED WARBLERS

This family of perching birds, often found in woodlands and reedbeds, can be hard to tell apart. Most species are olive-brown on their uppermost regions and yellow or beige below. Sometimes, it is the reed warbler's song, rather than the bird's features, that helps scientists and birdwatchers work out which species is which.

COMMON REED WARBLER
(Acrocephalus scirpaceus)

The female common reed warbler takes seven days to build its cup-shaped nest, hung above water in reedbeds. Made from trimmed grasses, reed stems, and leaves and lined with hair, including wool, the nest is almost impossible to spot.

The presence of a nest is often given away by the movement of parent birds, coming and going with food for the nestlings. Insects, especially those hatching from the surface of the water or those hiding among the reeds, are an important source of food for growing chicks.

LENGTH: 12–14 cm

DIET: Insects and, occasionally, berries

FOUND IN: Breeds in wetlands throughout Europe

AQUATIC WARBLER
(Acrocephalus paludicola)

Because insects can be very plentiful around water, the aquatic warbler is less territorial than other birds, and often individuals make nests very close to one another. This is because, with so much food around, it has less to fear from competition.

The male aquatic warbler plays almost no part in nesting. Instead, while the female feeds the chicks, the male finds a perch and repeats its churring song in an attempt to father more chicks. As with many warblers, the aquatic warbler can produce two sets of eggs each year, one in late spring and one in early summer.

LENGTH: 13 cm

DIET: Insects and spiders

FOUND IN: Breeds in wetlands across eastern Europe and western Asia

AFRICAN YELLOW WARBLER
(Iduna natalensis)

The African yellow warbler is an adaptable insect-hunter. It can leap into the air to catch flying termites, run like a mouse to catch scurrying beetles, or kick through leaves to expose woodlice and millipedes. Mostly, it does this under the cover of the undergrowth, rarely showing its face to humans.

During the breeding season, the African yellow warbler becomes less shy. The male regularly takes to an exposed perch, where it lets out its song—a repetitive "chup-chup chwee chwee chwee." Like many warblers, the African yellow warbler likes to sing from the same perch again and again.

LENGTH: 13 cm

DIET: Insects

FOUND IN: Thick undergrowth near water in parts of central and southern Africa

AUSTRALIAN REED WARBLER
(Acrocephalus australis)

To convince others of its nest-making skills, the male Australian reed warbler makes a fake nest at the start of the breeding season and shows it off to passing females. The mocked-up nest, which is too flimsy for real eggs, helps females work out which male is the highest quality individual in the local neighborhood.

Like many warblers, singing is another important part of the Australian reed warbler's courtship routine. The male's song is full of rich flute-like notes mixed with hard and metallic scratching noises.

LENGTH: 15–16 cm

DIET: Insects

FOUND IN: Densely vegetated wetlands across Australia

SHRIKES

These medium-sized birds are sometimes known as "butcherbirds" because they impale their prey on thorns and spines. This behavior, mostly undertaken by males, has two functions. One function is to save food for later; the other is to show off their hunting skills to nearby females.

GREAT GRAY SHRIKE
(Lanius excubitor)

The great gray shrike has a variety of calls, including crow-like alarm cries, birds-of-prey warning calls, and clunking chirps to alert nest mates that their hatchlings may be in danger. It is said that they can even mimic the calls of other birds, encouraging them out of the undergrowth so that they can be spotted and attacked.

Lacking sharp claws to help it tear apart its prey, the great gray shrike makes use of thorns or even the barbs of barbed wire to hold its prey in place. Once secure, the shrike tears its food apart using its beak. As well as eating birds, the great gray shrike has been known to eat larger prey, including bats, salamanders, and young stoats. Each animal is carefully left on its spike for eating later, ideally after other shrikes in the area have had a chance to notice the shrike's hunting skills. If a female considers the catch impressive, the male may be in with a good chance of securing a mate.

LENGTH: 24–25 cm

DIET: Mostly birds, mice, voles, lemmings, frogs, and lizards

FOUND IN: Open grasslands across Europe, Asia, and northern Africa

RED-BACKED SHRIKE
(Lanius collurio)

Being smaller than other shrikes, the red-backed shrike prefers to hunt large flying insects, rather than birds or mice. Dragonflies, beetles, hornets, and wasps are especially targeted, often chased in long aerial dogfights across the sky. When the kill has been made, the shrike returns to its treetop perch to look for its next meal.

Seasonal weather is important to the red-backed shrike. In hot summers, when there are especially high numbers of insects, a female shrike may have as many as eight hatchlings in the nest, many of whom will survive to adulthood.

LENGTH: 17–19 cm

DIET: Insects, birds, and small mammals

FOUND IN: Breeds in tree-dotted grasslands across Europe and western Asia

LOGGERHEAD SHRIKE
(Lanius ludovicianus)

This is the only shrike that lives in North America. Like other shrikes, the loggerhead shrike regularly scans the landscape from a high point in its territory, normally about 4 meters off the ground. Telephone wires are particularly favored.

Young loggerhead shrikes instinctively know how to impale their prey on thorns, needing no instruction from their parents. When they are adults, they tend to store mice and voles most of all. These "larders" provide important back-up food when bad weather stops them from hunting.

LENGTH: 21 cm

DIET: Insects and spiders, as well as small mammals, reptiles, and amphibians

FOUND IN: Tree-dotted grasslands across North America

STARLINGS

Starlings are very social birds that sometimes form large flocks before roosting in the evening. Their calls are long and often include noises and sounds incorporated from their environment. Some starlings in towns and cities include human words or car alarms in their songs.

COMMON STARLING
(Sturnus vulgaris)

To avoid being targeted by birds of prey, starlings form flocks that sometimes contain a million or more birds all flying together. When viewed up close, each starling in the flock can be seen to be copying the movement of those closest to it. When viewed from afar, the flock looks like a dark sphere that frequently expands and contracts into a variety of strange shapes in the sky.

Birdwatchers describe this unusual flocking behavior in starlings as a murmuration. In Denmark, it is known as a *sort sol*, which means "black sun" in English.

LENGTH: 19–23 cm

DIET: Mostly insects

FOUND IN: Towns and cities throughout the northern hemisphere

CAPE STARLING
(Lamprotornis nitens)

When it comes to finding food, the Cape starling is spoilt for choice. It knows where the best bird feeders are, where the finest fruiting trees are found, and the other birds it can track in order to be led to food. Sometimes, the Cape starling even eats ticks and fleas from large mammals.

During the breeding season, pairs of Cape starlings look for crevices in trees in which to build their nests. Because demand for nest-holes in spring is very high, much of the starling's energy is spent on aggressively defending its nest.

LENGTH: 25 cm

DIET: Mostly fruit and insects

FOUND IN: Woodlands, gardens, and urban areas of southern Africa

COMMON MYNA
(Acridotheres tristis)

Once an Asian species, the common myna is now found worldwide. It is one of the most invasive birds in the world. Its appetite for fruits in orchards and its habit of spreading weeds (through seeds in its droppings) has caused the species to be described as a pest by many farmers.

By aggressively scaring away nesting birds in its territory, the common myna is also capable of influencing the number and types of birds living in a habitat. Hole-nesting parrots, particularly, look elsewhere when there are mynas around.

LENGTH: 23–26 cm

DIET: Mostly fruits, grains, insects, and grubs

FOUND IN: Once in woodlands across Asia but now, introduced by humans, worldwide

HILDEBRANDT'S STARLING
(Lamprotornis hildebrandti)

Unlike most other starlings, the Hildebrandt's starling sometimes helps out at its parent's nest, assisting the family in rearing another batch of hatchlings. This special arrangement, known as cooperative breeding, is seen in about one in ten bird species.

Like many starlings, the wing feathers of the male Hildebrant's starling become noticeably shinier and more metallic during the breeding season. This so-called iridescence effect occurs because the texture of each feather reflects light in lots of different directions at once.

LENGTH: 18 cm

DIET: Mainly insects and seeds

FOUND IN: Open woodlands across Kenya and Tanzania

SUNBIRDS

Most sunbirds have a downward-curving beak and brush-tipped tongue for nectar feeding. As they move through the forest, they carry pollen from plant to plant, pollinating flowers as they go. Broadly, sunbirds do the same job in Africa and tropical Asia that hummingbirds perform in the Americas.

MALACHITE SUNBIRD
(Nectarinia famosa)

Like many sunbirds, the male and female malachite sunbird look very different. The male, particularly, uses its colored feathers to attract females. To draw extra attention to itself, the male sings a twittering song, while pointing its head upward to show off two tufts of yellow feathers on its chest.

Uniquely, the malachite sunbird also displays these tufts of feathers throughout the night while sleeping. Some scientists think it does this because the yellow feather tufts may look like a pair of eyes to any nocturnal predators watching nearby.

LENGTH: 13–27 cm

DIET: Nectar and insects

FOUND IN: Moorlands, forest edges, and gardens in Kenya, Malawi, and Zambia

SAHYADRI SUNBIRD
(Aethopyga vigorsii)

The nest of the Sahyadri sunbird resembles a purse. At its entrance is a flap-like "porch" decorated with objects such as tiny scraps of paper, fragments of bark, and even caterpillar droppings. The construction is held together using a mix of plant stems and spiderwebs.

Like other sunbirds, the Sahyadri sunbird flies fast through the tree canopy. When feeding from flowers it can hover briefly like a hummingbird. Mostly, however, it collects nectar by standing on a nearby twig.

LENGTH: 10–15 cm

DIET: Nectar and insects

FOUND IN: Forests and forest edges throughout India's Western Ghats

BLACK-BELLIED SUNBIRD
(Cinnyris nectarinioides)

The black-bellied sunbird is the smallest of all sunbirds. It zips through the forest canopy looking for exactly the right shape of flowers in which to dip its beak. If a flowering tree is particularly rich in nectar, the black-bellied sunbird will chase away insects drawn to the sweet smell. Large bees, in particular, are aggressively forced off its turf.

As it feeds, the black-bellied sunbird nervously watches for passing birds of prey. To keep safe, these small sunbirds work together with other birds to "mob" predators and urge them away from their territories.

LENGTH: 10–13 cm

DIET: Nectar, insects, and spiders

FOUND IN: Savannas across Ethiopia, Kenya, Somalia, and Tanzania

SPECTACLED SPIDERHUNTER
(Arachnothera flavigaster)

Almost the size of a blackbird, the spectacled spiderhunter is the largest of all sunbirds. As the name suggests, this bird sometimes collects spiders, landing on nearby twigs and using its long beak to reach over and pluck them from their webs. As with other sunbirds, however, most of its energy comes from nectar.

The nest of the spectacled spiderhunter differs from other sunbirds. Each nest, barely the size of a teacup, has a spout-like entrance hole weaved from crushed, dried leaves, held together with spiderwebs.

LENGTH: 21–22 cm

DIET: Spiders, insects, and nectar

FOUND IN: Forests of Brunei, Indonesia, Malaysia, Singapore, Thailand, and Vietnam

SWALLOWS, MARTINS, AND SAW-WINGS

These perching birds, collectively known as hirundines, are among the fastest and most dynamic of all birds. A streamlined body shape helps hirundines zip through the air after flying insects, their favorite food.

BARN SWALLOW
(Hirundo rustica)

Like all hirundines, the barn swallow resembles a fighter jet. Its lightweight and aerodynamic body means that it can quickly switch direction when chasing prey. Its wing shape also saves energy: Swallows burn only half as much energy as birds of a similar size while flying.

The barn swallow's long tail feathers (known as streamers) are especially important to males. Females use the length of the males' streamers to work out which are the most desirable mates in the area. The longer the streamers, the more interested in nest-building the female tends to be.

LENGTH: 17–19 cm

DIET: Insects

FOUND IN: Meadows and farmlands throughout the northern hemisphere

LESSER STRIPED SWALLOW
(Cecropis abyssinica)

Like other swallows, the lesser striped swallow builds a nest from pellets of mud collected from wetlands and then crafted into a cup-like shape attached to a cave or cliff wall. Inside, its eggs rest on a thin layer of grasses. Swallow nests are often used again and again.

In modern times, swallows of many different species regularly seek out human buildings as places to make their nests. As well as nesting on the sides of tall buildings, the lesser striped swallow also builds its nest upon bridges and tunnels.

LENGTH: 15–19 cm

DIET: Insects

FOUND IN: Woodlands across the southern half of Africa

WHITE-EYED RIVER MARTIN
(Pseudochelidon sirintarae)

This wetland martin has a wide mouth, suitable for snapping at insects mid-flight, and larger eyes than other martins. Some scientists think its large eyes may suggest the white-eyed river martin hunts at night, when light is scarce. This may explain why it is so rare and hard to spot.

No-one has seen or heard a white-eyed river martin for more than forty years, but there is hope that this species is not yet extinct. Some scientists think that it may survive in remote parts of Thailand. To this day, the search continues.

LENGTH: 15 cm

FOUND IN: Rivers in remote parts of Thailand

DIET: Insects

FANTI SAW-WING
(Psalidoprocne obscura)

With its shimmering blue-green feathers, the fanti saw-wing is the most eye-catching of all swallows. With a slow, sometimes gliding, flight it patrols patches of grasslands, often near water, searching for large beetles in flight.

As with other hirundines, the eyeballs of the fanti saw-wing are large and well-equipped for keeping track of objects moving fast through the sky. This allows them to keep focus on flying insects when they are very close by, dodging and weaving to escape the snapping beak.

LENGTH: 17 cm

DIET: Flying insects, especially beetles

FOUND IN: Woodlands, forest edges, and grasslands across southern West Africa

TANAGERS

The insect-hunting strategies of tanagers are very varied. Some tanagers probe for grubs in soil, some turn over leaves for spiders, and others hunt from perches to catch insects mid-flight. Almost 400 tanager species are known, making this one of the largest families of perching birds.

SWALLOW TANAGER
(Tersina viridis)

When courting, swallow tanagers regularly bow toward one another. They also engage in bouts of hopping and chasing as if playing a game. During these activities, the female attempts to work out whether the male is of good enough quality to nest with.

While most tanagers make a cup-shaped nest, the female swallow tanager sometimes digs a burrow or uses existing holes in stone buildings, riverbanks, or under bridges. Though males are protective of their nests, they do not defend a large territory like other birds.

LENGTH: 14–15 cm

DIET: Fruits, insects, and spiders

FOUND IN: Forests across South America, from Panama to Argentina

BANANAQUIT
(Coereba flaveola)

As with sunbirds, the tongue of the bananaquit is adapted to help scoop nectar from flowerheads. Wide, long, and oar-like, it can be pressed deep into flowering plants and sometimes into bananas. If a flowerhead is too deep for its beak, the bananaquit has been known to puncture the base of the flower with its beak to steal the nectar directly from the plant.

Unlike hummingbirds, the bananaquit is unable to hover. For this reason, it always feeds while perched on nearby branches.

LENGTH: 10–11 cm

DIET: Nectar, fruits, and small insects

FOUND IN: Forests, gardens, and parks throughout South America and parts of the Caribbean and the Himalayas

WHITE-CAPPED TANAGER
(Sericossypha albocristata)

The white-capped tanager is one of the noisiest of all tanagers. Its shrieking calls are often performed simultaneously by many members of the flock at once and sometimes go on for ten minutes at a time.

In years of study, scientists have only ever seen one single white-capped tanager nest. About the size of a plate, the nest contained a single fledgling, tended to by lots of adults. This suggests that the white-capped tanager is a "cooperative breeder," with family members that stick around the nest to help rear another round of hatchlings.

LENGTH: 24 cm

DIET: Seeds, fruits, and insects

FOUND IN: Forests throughout Colombia, Venezuela, Ecuador, and Peru

VAMPIRE GROUND FINCH
(Geospiza septentrionalis)

This island-dwelling tanager is well-named. When it cannot find other sources of food, it hops up to large seabirds and pecks at their skin to release drops of blood, which it laps up. Strangely, when this happens, seabirds do not chase the vampire ground finch away. Scientists think this is because, rather than drinking blood, the seabirds think this tanager is pecking at pests, including feather mites and ticks, that live on its skin. The vampire ground finch is also fond of eating seabirds' eggs, which it smashes open by rolling them onto jagged rocks.

LENGTH: 11–12 cm

DIET: Insects, fruits, seeds, bird eggs, and blood

FOUND IN: Northwestern Galapagos Islands

THRUSHES

These small to medium-sized birds are often found hopping on the floor in wooded areas. As well as eating insects, thrushes like to eat worms, which they pull from the ground using their beak. Some thrushes also like to eat snails, smashing their shells on rocks to get to their juicy insides. Their cup-shaped nests are sometimes lined with mud.

EURASIAN BLACKBIRD
(Turdus merula)

Blasted into the sky from a high perch, the blackbird's rich and fluty song is unmistakable. Unlike many birds, which often sing for only a few weeks each year, the male blackbird sings for months on end. In human cultures, its songs have inspired poetry, myths, and folklore.

As well as singing, the Eurasian blackbird also has many different alarm calls to warn others around them of potential dangers. One call, which sounds like a "pook-pook-pook," is used when cats are around. Another common call is a high-pitched "seeeeeee…" used when birds of prey fly overhead.

LENGTH: 24–27 cm

DIET: Insects, earthworms, seeds, and berries

FOUND IN: Woodlands across Eurasia, North Africa, and South Asia

GREAT THRUSH
(Turdus fuscater)

Planted high up in trees or tall bushes, the great thrush's cup-nest is dressed with carefully cut twigs, mosses, and stringy bark stripped from trees. Like many thrushes, its eggs are a striking green-blue color with lots of spots.

For more than a century, scientists have argued about why the eggs of some birds, especially thrushes, are so decorated. Many now agree that the color is probably an adaptation that helps parents recognize which eggs belong to them, and which eggs belong to nest parasites, such as cuckoos.

LENGTH: 28–30 cm

DIET: Fruits, snails, worms, and insects

FOUND IN: Forests, gardens, and farmlands throughout the Andes mountain range in South America

WESTERN BLUEBIRD
(Sialia mexicana)

The beak of the western bluebird is not long or tough enough to make holes in trees, so it scours woodlands looking for empty woodpecker holes to nest in. In spring, there is lots of competition for old woodpecker holes. Western bluebirds regularly fight with other hole-nesting birds, including tree swallows, sparrows, and starlings, for places to nest.

To ease this competition, scientists sometimes make wooden nest-boxes and hang them on trees or buildings. By making the entrance hole just the right size, bluebirds can be protected from nest-raiding predators, including cats, raccoons, and birds of prey.

LENGTH: 17–19 cm

DIET: Insects, fruits, and seeds

FOUND IN: Woodlands, forests, and farmlands across western parts of Central and North America

FRUIT-HUNTER
(Chlamydochaera jefferyi)

While sitting on eggs, the female fruit-hunter accepts a variety of fruits specially collected by the male. These include figs and white lemon-scented berries from laurel shrubs.

Many of the seeds contained within the fruit-hunter's food pass through its gut undigested and are released in its droppings. This helps seeds get to new parts of the forest. Seeds have other tricks to help them spread. Some seeds are especially furry so that they get stuck to bird feathers. When the bird next cleans its feathers, these seeds drop to the floor and begin to grow.

LENGTH: 23 cm

DIET: Fruits, berries, and snails

FOUND IN: Forests of Borneo in Southeast Asia

TITS, TITMICE, AND CHICKADEES

These nimble and social birds live in woodlands across the northern hemisphere. They use a small, stout beak to eat a range of foods, including seeds and insects, especially caterpillars. Though small in size, this group of perching birds are among the most brainy of all birds. Many have adapted quickly to human towns and cities.

SULTAN TIT
(Melanochlora sultanea)

The sultan tit is the largest of all in this group. Its size means it can grab at bigger prey than other tits, such as grasshoppers, spiders, and even praying mantises. Like many tits, the sultan tit often hunts in large, noisy groups, sometimes numbering ten or more. Sometimes these groups mix with other bird species, especially babblers.

When predators, such as birds of prey, come close, the sultan tit flicks up a dazzling yellow crest above its head. This warns the predator that it has been spotted and its attempt to catch the tit has failed.

LENGTH: 20–21 cm

DIET: Mostly insects

FOUND IN: Forests throughout South and Southeast Asia

EURASIAN BLUE TIT
(Cyanistes caeruleus)

Dangling acrobatically off twigs, the Eurasian blue tit can catch 100 or more caterpillars in a day. Many of these it takes back to its hungry chicks. Feeding chicks, often ten or more, keeps the Eurasian blue tit very busy. At the peak of spring, an adult blue tit may be in and out of the nest with food every ninety seconds.

Rather than migrate south during the winter, many Eurasian blue tits stay in their habitats all year. To keep warm, blue tits huddle together at night in tree-holes or wooden nest-boxes.

LENGTH: 11–12 cm

DIET: Insects, fruits, and seeds

FOUND IN: Woodlands, parks, and gardens throughout Europe and parts of the Middle East

BRIDLED TITMOUSE
(Baeolophus wollweberi)

The bridled titmouse is a bird with many voices. During the breeding season, the male sings a ten-minute dawn serenade to females while they sit on eggs. Males also have a "chick-a-dee" call used to defend territories. Females call back to males regularly, with purring sounds often delivered while gently vibrating their wings.

The bridled titmouse's chicks often join in the conversation. Before they fledge, chicks produce an insect-like buzzing sound that encourages the parents to continue to give them food. Bugs and beetles are an especially common source of food.

LENGTH: 10 cm

DIET: Mostly insects

FOUND IN: Oak woodlands throughout western USA and Mexico

GRAY-HEADED CHICKADEE
(Poecile cinctus)

Because it lives in a cooler climate, the mountain chickadee frequently sunbathes to gather enough warmth needed for hunting. Like a solar panel, it opens its wings slightly and turns to face the sun.

Living in forests that change a lot during the seasons, the gray-headed chickadee alters its diet regularly, according to what food is most available. Springtime sees the mountain chickadee focus on caterpillars and beetles, whereas summer sees this species move on to aphids and stinkbugs. Conifer seeds get the mountain chickadee through winter months when insects become hard to find.

LENGTH: 13–14 cm

DIET: Insects, spiders, and seeds

FOUND IN: Coniferous forests across the northern hemisphere

TYRANT FLYCATCHERS

With more than 400 species, the tyrant flycatchers are the largest family of perching birds. Though the two groups are not closely related, tyrants and other flycatchers have lots in common. Their songs are less complicated than those of other perching birds, and their diet is mostly made up of insects.

VERMILION FLYCATCHER
(Pyrocephalus obscurus)

The vermilion flycatcher's cup-shaped nest is not much larger than the lid of a jam-jar. Mosses, tiny twigs, and spiderwebs are just some of the ingredients it uses for its nest, as well as hair, feathers and human-made items, including bits of string.

Almost one in five of the eggs laid in a vermilion flycatcher's nest is put there by a rival female. Known as "brood parasitism," this behavior means unrelated female flycatchers can trick others into raising their babies, saving them lots of energy.

LENGTH: 13–14 cm

DIET: Insects, especially flies, grasshoppers, and beetles

FOUND IN: Savannas and open patches of woodland in South America, Central America, and southern states of the USA

BROWN-CRESTED FLYCATCHER
(Myiarchus tyrannulus)

Close to the size of a blackbird, the brown-crested flycatcher is one of the largest of all tyrant flycatchers. Using spectacular flying skills, this flycatcher has been known to catch larger prey than just insects, including small lizards and even hummingbirds.

During the breeding season, the male brown-crested flycatcher uses its talent for aerial acrobatics to show off to females. Once they have chosen each other, male and female make a nest in a hole in an old tree trunk, lined with fur stolen from dead animals and pieces of shed snakeskin.

LENGTH: 18–23 cm

DIET: Mostly insects

FOUND IN: Breeds in open woodlands in southern California, southern Nevada, central Arizona, and southern Texas

YELLOWISH FLYCATCHER

(Empidonax flavescens)

The yellowish flycatcher is quick and graceful. As it moves from place to place, it takes insects from twigs and leaves, occasionally dashing into the air to pick them off as they try to fly away.

This small, secretive flycatcher often hides among branches in dense, low-growing trees. Like many tyrant flycatchers, this species depends heavily on camouflage to protect itself from predators. Its simple song, often repeated over and over again, is a high-pitched "see … seeeeen… chit." This song has been heard being performed for a full fifteen minutes before the sun rises.

LENGTH: 14 cm

DIET: Insects and, less commonly, fruits

FOUND IN: Breeds in highlands across scattered parts of Central America

MANY-COLORED RUSH TYRANT

(Tachuris rubrigastra)

The many-colored rush tyrant lives up to its name. During the nesting season, the male shows off its colorful feathers to females, who watch from the banks of rivers and streams. Its insect-like song is full of buzzing and gurgling notes.

The nest of the many-colored rush tyrant resembles an upturned thimble. Attached to a single reed, it is held in place using wet pieces of leaves that harden like cement as they dry. Its nests are both camouflaged and, dangling on a wobbly reed, hard for predators to climb into.

LENGTH: 11–12 cm

DIET: Insects

FOUND IN: Marshlands and reedbeds of southern South America

WAXBILLS AND ALLIES

Scientists have put waxbills together with manakins, firefinches, parrotfinches, and others into a group known as the estrildid finches. Though these birds are not closely related to true finches, they have many of the same features as finches, including the short, thick beak used for opening seeds.

ORANGE-CHEEKED WAXBILL
(Estrilda melpoda)

Like an acrobat, the orange-cheeked waxbill dodges through branches and scurries up and down tree trunks. While feeding among grasses, it regularly dangles upside down from nearby twigs to get at seeds.

During the nesting season, the male orange-cheeked waxbill carefully selects a tender stem of grass and holds it in its beak, which it points to the sky. It then begins to bob up and down, singing a shrieky song, while edging closer and closer toward the watching female. Grass seeds are used to camouflage the nest, found close by.

LENGTH: 10 cm

DIET: Small grass seeds and insects

FOUND IN: Grasslands throughout central and western Africa

BEAUTIFUL FIRETAIL
(Stagonopleura bella)

The beautiful firetail is well-named, although seeing one in the wild is difficult. This small bird feeds on grasses that are low to the ground, and frequently disappears into the undergrowth when predators are around, especially pet cats.

Like other estrildid finches, the nest of the beautiful firetail is carefully constructed. Built like a glass bottle, it has a long, tunnel entrance, woven from grasses and small twigs, which opens out into a fist-sized sphere that is filled with tiny feathers to insulate the chicks.

LENGTH: 11 cm

DIET: Seeds, small insects, and snails

FOUND IN: Shrublands and coastal heathlands of southeastern Australia

WAXWINGS

Waxwings are a small group of birds named for their red wingtips, which look like the special red wax once used to seal envelopes. Well known for their dazzling feather patterns and eye-catching crests, these birds often gather together in trees and bushes to devour berries.

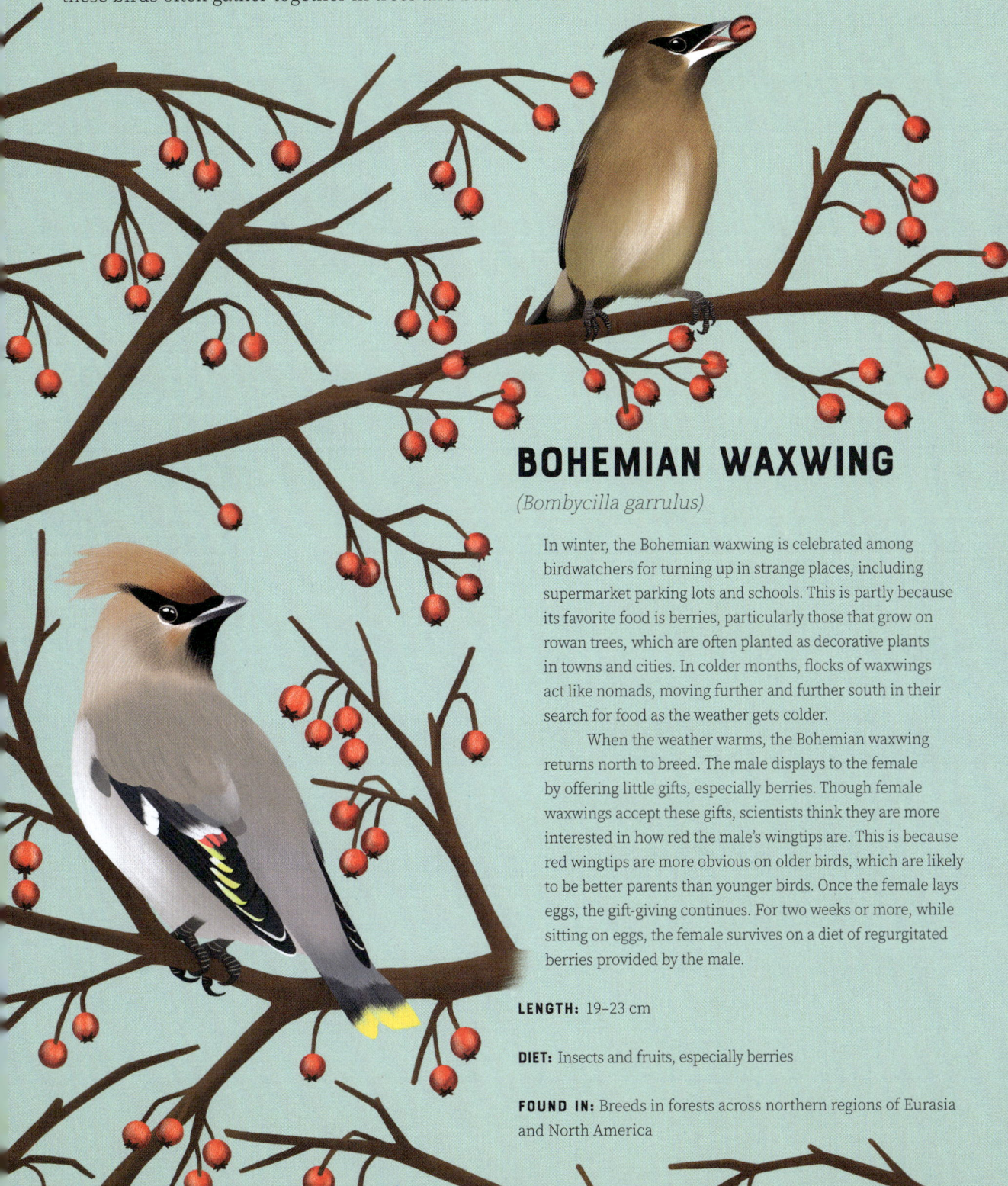

BOHEMIAN WAXWING
(Bombycilla garrulus)

In winter, the Bohemian waxwing is celebrated among birdwatchers for turning up in strange places, including supermarket parking lots and schools. This is partly because its favorite food is berries, particularly those that grow on rowan trees, which are often planted as decorative plants in towns and cities. In colder months, flocks of waxwings act like nomads, moving further and further south in their search for food as the weather gets colder.

When the weather warms, the Bohemian waxwing returns north to breed. The male displays to the female by offering little gifts, especially berries. Though female waxwings accept these gifts, scientists think they are more interested in how red the male's wingtips are. This is because red wingtips are more obvious on older birds, which are likely to be better parents than younger birds. Once the female lays eggs, the gift-giving continues. For two weeks or more, while sitting on eggs, the female survives on a diet of regurgitated berries provided by the male.

LENGTH: 19–23 cm

DIET: Insects and fruits, especially berries

FOUND IN: Breeds in forests across northern regions of Eurasia and North America

WEAVERS

Weavers get their name from their habit of making nests from grass stems that are woven together and hung from trees. These birds nest in noisy communities that consist of many nests packed tightly together. A weaver's nest has an entrance hole in the bottom, which makes it harder for predators to climb or slither into.

VILLAGE WEAVER
(Ploceus cucullatus)

A single village weaver nest is made from about 300 blades of grass, each carefully trimmed and put in place one by one by the male. If impressed with the construction, the female collects feathers and pieces of palm leaves to line the inside.

In the breeding season, a single tree can become home to more than fifty village weaver nests. Throughout the day, weavers come and go with food for chicks, making lots of noise. Village weavers are known to make twenty different calls. Many of these calls alert colonies to approaching predators, such as snakes.

LENGTH: 17 cm

FOUND IN: Many habitats across sub-Saharan Africa

DIET: Mostly seeds and insects

RED-BILLED QUELEA
(Quelea quelea)

With an estimated population of more than a billion birds, the red-billed quelea is thought to be the most numerous wild bird in the world. It regularly forms flocks that contain millions of birds, which move like a rolling cloud across the landscape. Because this weaver can devour farmers' crops, some call it the "feathered locust."

In the red-billed quelea's breeding season, finding grass seeds at just the right time to eat, as they ripen, can be difficult. To gather enough of this food for its young, the red-billed quelea has to fly more than 30 or 40 miles each day.

LENGTH: 12 cm

FOUND IN: Many habitats across sub-Saharan Africa

DIET: Seeds and insects

WHITE-HEADED BUFFALO WEAVER
(Dinemellia dinemelli)

Unlike other weavers, the white-headed buffalo weaver makes a nest by compacting grasses together instead of weaving. First, using dry grass stems and feathers, it constructs an inner nest chamber, and then it adds an armored layer to the outside, made from thorny twigs and branches. This keeps predators at bay.

White-headed buffalo weaver nests are so well-constructed that other birds regularly investigate them when they are empty and lay their own eggs inside. Pygmy falcons are especially dependent on white-headed buffalo weaver nests to help raise their young.

LENGTH: 18 cm

DIET: Mostly insects

FOUND IN: Savannas across Ethiopia, Kenya, Somalia, Sudan, Tanzania, and Uganda

SOCIABLE WEAVER
(Philetairus socius)

The sociable weaver builds the largest of all bird nests. Its communal nests, some 7 meters or so in length, look like giant haystacks hung in the branches of thorny trees. Inside, sociable weaver nests contain numerous chambers, each of which is used by a nesting pair. On cool nights, weavers gather in chambers in the middle of the structure to keep warm.

Other egg-laying animals make use of sociable weaver nests, including birds of prey, lizards, and snakes. Underneath these nests, many different species of beetles gather to feast on the constant supply of nutritious droppings the weavers produce.

LENGTH: 14 cm

DIET: Mostly insects

FOUND IN: Dry countrysides throughout southwestern Africa

WHITE-EYES

These small birds with white-rimmed eyes are found across Africa, Asia, and Australasia. Unlike other species, white-eyes are flexible about the foods they eat. Using this skill, they adapt quickly to living on islands, which contain fewer plants and animals than mainland habitats. For this reason, white-eyes are found on lots of tropical islands, especially in the Indian Ocean and the western Pacific Ocean.

SILVEREYE
(Zosterops lateralis)

Hanging from a branch among lots of dense leaves, the silvereye's nest is almost impossible to spot. About the size of a teacup, it is made from moss, spiderwebs, and stringy fibers pulled from thistles. Animal hair, sometimes plucked from barbed wire, provides extra insulation for its hatchlings.

Silvereyes regularly migrate to warmer climates in winter, often traveling thousands of miles at a time. In cold years, when food becomes especially scarce, the silvereye has been known to raid garden birdfeeders, where it is fond of sugary water, bread, and solid lumps of fat left out by bird-lovers.

LENGTH: 12 cm

DIET: Insects, worms, spiders, fruits, berries, and nectar

FOUND IN: Many habitats across Australia, New Zealand, and nearby islands

MOUNTAIN BLACKEYE
(Zosterops emiliae)

The mountain blackeye lives in the most remote and hilly parts of Borneo. Only in long periods of drought, when it becomes desperate for water, does it stray down to lower altitudes.

When searching for food, the mountain blackeye occasionally visits special bowl-like plants known as pitcher plants. When feeding on the plant's nectar, the mountain blackeye sometimes releases its droppings, which fall into the plant's "bowl" and are digested. This kind of relationship, where both animal and plant benefit, is known as mutualistic.

LENGTH: 11–12 cm

FOUND IN: The summits of Borneo's highest mountains

DIET: Nectar, pollen, insects, and small berries

GOLDEN WHITE-EYE
(Cleptornis marchei)

The golden white-eye tolerates no intruders. It regularly bullies smaller white-eyes off its turf, hounding them by flapping its wings and tapping them with its beak until they move on. If a flock of rival white-eyes should fly through its patch, the golden white-eye flies directly through the middle of the flock to try to disperse it.

Hidden in foliage about 3 meters from the ground, the nest of the golden white-eye is made from pine needles, grasses, and stringy vines. Its hatchlings are targeted by many predators, including starlings, kingfishers, and climbing, lizard-like reptiles known as skinks.

LENGTH: 14 cm

DIET: Fruits, berries, and insects

FOUND IN: The Northern Mariana Islands in the western Pacific Ocean

BONIN WHITE-EYE
(Apalopteron familiare)

Living on the Bonin Islands south of Japan, this white-eye has adapted quickly to island life by feeding on a range of foods, from fruits to flowers and insects. By passing seeds through its body in its droppings, this bird helps forest plants spread across its environment.

For many years, scientists thought that the secretive Bonin white-eye had no true song. However, more recent expeditions in its island habitats have revealed that it does sing, but only for a short period just before the sun rises over the horizon.

LENGTH: 12–14 cm

DIET: Fruits, flowers, and insects

FOUND IN: Many habitats throughout the Bonin Islands

WHYDAHS, INDIGOBIRDS, AND CUCKOO-FINCHES

Together, these perching birds are known as viduids. This small bird group, which contains just twenty species, do not make their own nests. Instead, they lay their eggs in the nests of other species.

PIN-TAILED WHYDAH
(Vidua macroura)

During the breeding season, the male pin-tailed whydah does all it can to show off its long tail feathers. During its courtship display, it bounces through the air in a circle, momentarily hovering above the female's face so that its tail decorations cannot be avoided. While displaying, the male utters a chittering call that is sometimes aimed at other birds, like canaries and shrikes, that dare come too close. Should the female accept the male's advances, the pair visit a special patch of grass and feed together before the female looks for a suitable nest for its eggs.

The female pin-tailed whydah often lays its eggs in waxbill nests. When a waxbill nest is left unattended, the female sneaks in and eats one of the eggs to make room for its own. The female then lays a single egg and later returns to deliver more. In a good year, the female pin-tailed whydah may lay as many as twenty eggs in other birds' nests using this strategy.

LENGTH: 11–32 cm

DIET: Grass seeds and, occasionally, insects

FOUND IN: Grasslands and savannas across central and southern Africa

VILLAGE INDIGOBIRD
(Vidua chalybeata)

During the breeding season, the village indigobird is especially watchful for the comings and goings of firefinches attending to their nests. When the firefinches leave a nest, even if just for a moment, the indigobird takes its chance to sneak in an egg or two.

To make sure its eggs go unnoticed by its host, the female indigobird lays eggs that match the firefinches' eggs closely. Indigobird hatchlings also mimic the look of firefinch chicks, especially when they have their mouths open to beg for food.

LENGTH: 10–11 cm

DIET: Grass seeds and, occasionally, insects

FOUND IN: Open woodlands and villages across central and southern Africa

CUCKOO-WEAVER
(Anomalospiza imberbis)

Before laying its egg, the female cuckoo-weaver does its best to remove other eggs from the nest of its host, often letting them fall to the ground. This makes this species more destructive than its close relatives, the indigobirds and whydahs. The cuckoo-weaver favors nests made by small, insect-eating birds.

Fed wasps and caterpillars by their new foster parents, cuckoo-weaver chicks grow quickly. They fledge the nest just two weeks after hatching, and continue to be fed for another three weeks or more by their devoted hosts.

LENGTH: 11–12 cm

DIET: Seeds and, occasionally, insects

FOUND IN: Woodlands and grasslands across central and southern Africa

WOODSWALLOWS, BUTCHERBIRDS, AND CURRAWONGS

These perching birds, known as artamids, have stocky beaks. In some species, the beaks are slightly hooked, like a falcon's. They are known for forming tight groups at night, which cluster together on branches to keep warm. Twenty-four artamid species have so far been discovered, living across Australasia and southern parts of Asia.

WHITE-BREASTED WOODSWALLOW
(Artamus leucorynchus)

The white-breasted woodswallow is a team player. Each year, young birds regularly help their parents to raise another batch of chicks, finding food for them while keeping the nest safe from rivals. Occasionally, if an insect is too large for one white-breasted woodswallow to eat, family members share their meals.

Should large predators, such as birds of prey, come close to a nest, woodswallow family groups bully them from their patch. They fly fast and aggressively, eventually stressing the predator out so much that it moves elsewhere to look for food.

LENGTH: 17–20 cm
DIET: Insects
FOUND IN: Open countrysides throughout southeastern Asian islands and Australia

FIJI WOODSWALLOW
(Artamus mentalis)

Like a miniature falcon, the Fiji woodswallow looks down from its hunting perch. Should it see a passing insect, it dashes downward to catch it in its slightly curved beak. Smaller insects are swallowed mid-air, while larger prey are taken back to the perch, where they are pulled apart with the woodswallow's beak and claws.

Like other woodswallows, the Fiji woodswallow is very social. As well as clustering together at night to keep warm, individuals sometimes feed injured family members, providing them with enough food to help them recover from injury or illness.

LENGTH: 17 cm
DIET: Flying insects
FOUND IN: Moist forests and savannas throughout many Fijian islands

GRAY BUTCHERBIRD
(Cracticus torquatus)

Like a stealthy assassin, the gray butcherbird silently approaches flocks of small birds while they forage for seeds. Before these birds even have time to whistle an alarm call, the gray butcherbird ambushes, striking its prey firmly in the head with a sharp bill that kills it instantly. Its meal is either eaten all at once or taken to a nearby tree and stored.

Like shrikes, the gray butcherbird can impale its food on a spike to be eaten later, hence the name "butcherbird."

LENGTH: 27–30 cm

FOUND IN: Forests and woodlands across Australia

DIET: Insects, small birds, fruits, seeds, and nectar

BLACK CURRAWONG
(Strepera fuliginosa)

Like a crow, the black currawong uses many approaches to find food. Some individuals pick at crustaceans hiding in seaweed or pull apart damp logs looking for grubs. Others strike at small birds that stray into their path. Dead birds are sometimes wedged into cracks between rocks and then pulled apart by the currawong tugging with its sturdy beak.

Like their close relatives, the black currawong is a very social bird. Individuals frequently engage in playful games, sometimes wrestling or rolling onto their backs and flicking and juggling fruits with their feet.

LENGTH: 50 cm

FOUND IN: Forests of Tasmania

DIET: Mainly insects, but also lizards, birds, mice, fruits, and seeds

WRENS

Most wrens are small and inconspicuous, only giving away their presence through a loud and startling song. Eighty-eight different kinds of these perching birds have been named, mostly from the Americas. Often, wrens have wings with little stripes on them and they run with their tail held high over the head.

GIANT WREN
(Campylorhynchus chiapensis)

About the same size and weight of a robin, the giant wren is one of the largest wrens in the world. It hunts close to the ground and is very watchful for predators. Though it eats insects, the giant wren has been known to enter chicken coops to try to eat their eggs.

Like other wrens, the giant wren builds a ball-shaped nest, constructed mostly from dried grasses, weed stems, and tangled, stringy vines. About the size of a sofa cushion, this nest is about twice as big as other wren nests.

LENGTH: 20–22 cm

DIET: Mostly insects

FOUND IN: Farmyards, hedgerows, and fruit orchards throughout parts of Mexico and Guatemala

COBB'S WREN
(Troglodytes cobbi)

Running up and down the shoreline of its island home, the Cobb's wren searches for shrimps and sea-lice washed onto shore after high tide. If spooked, this wren rarely flies. Instead, it prefers to dash toward nearby boulders and hide in cracks and crevices that predators cannot squeeze between.

When singing, the Cobb's wren stands upon the tallest boulders to make sure its voice can be heard over the noise of waves crashing on the beach. Its nest is carefully lined with seabird feathers and hair plucked from sleeping seals.

LENGTH: 13–14 cm

DIET: Insects and crustaceans

FOUND IN: Thick grasses and washed-up seaweeds throughout the Falkland Islands

EURASIAN WREN
(Troglodytes troglodytes)

For its size, the Eurasian wren has a voice box ten times more powerful than that of many other birds. During spring, it sings a loud and piercing burst of trills and sharp notes, delivered from an exposed perch. The effort of singing is so intense for wrens that they often appear to tremble as they sing.

During the breeding season, the male Eurasian wren also builds a range of neat, dome-shaped nests in its territory. Once constructed, the male encourages visiting females to look around each one to choose the nest it likes best. Often, the more nests a male constructs, the better its chances of finding a mate and raising chicks.

Freezing temperatures regularly cause wrens to roost together at night to keep warm. Occasionally, garden birdboxes can be used for this purpose. Sometimes, up to sixty wrens can gather inside a single birdbox, all snuggled up tightly against one another.

LENGTH: 9–10 cm

DIET: Insects, spiders, and some seeds

FOUND IN: Woodlands, hedgerows, and gardens throughout Europe, Asia, and northern Africa

MONARCH FLYCATCHERS

Found throughout Africa, Asia, and Australasia, this group of insect-eating birds is renowned for its cup-shaped nests, which are often found at the base of tree branches. Many monarch flycatchers purposefully place their nests near the nests of larger, more aggressive birds. This makes predators think twice about raiding them.

MALAGASY PARADISE FLYCATCHER
(Terpsiphone mutata)

Sparrowhawks, kites, and harrier hawks are just some of the predators that regularly hunt this colorful flycatcher. To guard against attack, the Malagasy paradise flycatcher regularly forms flocks with other insect-eating birds. By hanging around at the back of these flocks, it catches the insects fleeing from the birds at the front.

Even though its canopy nest is inaccessible to most predators, the Malagasy paradise flycatcher remains watchful while incubating its eggs. Larger animals known to attack its nests include snakes and monkey-like lemurs.

LENGTH: 18–36 cm, including tail

DIET: Flying insects

FOUND IN: Forests of Madagascar, Mayotte, and the Comoro Islands

INDIAN PARADISE FLYCATCHER
(Terpsiphone paradisi)

The Indian paradise flycatcher catches more than flies. Large insects such as praying mantises, giant grasshoppers, and swallowtail butterflies regularly feature in its diet. To stop these large insects fighting back, the Indian paradise flycatcher bashes its prey repeatedly against a rock, before tearing off the wings and eating the soft parts.

Like many paradise flycatchers, prey is spotted from special perches in the canopy and then chased and caught mid-air. These perches are often used again and again by the Indian paradise flycatcher.

LENGTH: 20–50 cm, including tail

DIET: Insects

FOUND IN: Tropical forests throughout central and South Asia

SCIMITAR BABBLERS

With their downward-curving bills, bright colors and charismatic floppy tails, the scimitar babblers are hard to miss. Their unusual beaks are used to move leaves, under which insects like to hide. In total, seventeen species are known, most of which live in tropical parts of Asia.

INDIAN SCIMITAR BABBLER
(Pomatorhinus horsfieldii)

The Indian scimitar babbler often feeds in groups of up to ten, which produce lots of calls that serve to keep the group together and alert for danger. These calls include bubbling sounds, hoots, chirps, and rattling noises.

Another sign that babblers are nearby is the crispy sound of leaves being tossed around to expose prey hiding underneath. Occasionally, if grubs attempt to escape by retreating into the ground, the Indian scimitar babbler turns up the soil aggressively, using its beak like a shovel.

LENGTH: 22 cm

FOUND IN: Tropical forests in India

DIET: Insects, spiders, and, occasionally, berries and nectar

SRI LANKA SCIMITAR BABBLER
(Pomatorhinus melanurus)

As it bursts off the forest floor and scampers up a tree trunk to get back to its nest, the Sri Lanka scimitar babbler resembles a small woodpecker. Its nest is an untidy platform of mosses, trimmed grass, and dead leaves, squashed into a crevice between tree branches. Very little is known about its courtship behaviors.

Because it appears on postage stamps in Sri Lanka, this scimitar babbler is well known. In the Sinhala-speaking community, it is called *parandel kurulla*, which translates as "dried-grass colored bird."

LENGTH: 19–21 cm

FOUND IN: Hill regions of Sri Lanka

DIET: Insects and spiders

TYPICAL ANTBIRDS

These small perching birds with round wings and strong legs are found in woodlands and forests of Central and South America. Many antbird species have tough-looking beaks, sometimes with a hooked tip used for holding and pulling apart insects. In total, more than 200 species are known.

BARRED ANTSHRIKE
(Thamnophilus doliatus)

Like many antbirds, the barred antshrike spends much of its time tracking swarms of army ants as they move through the forest. As well as picking off ants from the colony itself, the barred antshrike also takes out small animals trying to get out of the way of the advancing swarm. These include small lizards, stick insects, grasshoppers, and mantises.

The presence of antshrikes is often given away by their call, a chuckling "hu-hu-hu-hu" song, sometimes delivered by both male and female at the same time.

LENGTH: 15–18 cm

DIET: Mostly insects, berries, and small lizards

FOUND IN: Dense forests across Central and South America

OCELLATED ANTBIRD
(Phaenostictus mcleannani)

The ocellated antbird watches other antbirds to learn where the biggest colonies of army ants are located in the forest. When approaching a swarm of ants, the ocellated antbird fights off smaller antbirds to take prime position at the front of the colony, where it is easiest to catch insects running or flying away from the ants.

Like other antbirds, the ocellated antbird is watchful for predators that also gather near swarms of army ants, including wild cats. When threatened, this antbird regularly flicks its tail or lets out chirping calls that let predators know they are being watched.

LENGTH: 17–20 cm

DIET: Insects, spiders, and small lizards

FOUND IN: Forests in southern Central America and northern South America

OXPECKERS

Oxpeckers are known for their habit of sitting on zebras, giraffes, and other large African mammals, searching for ticks and fleas to eat. These large animals struggle to rid themselves of these insect pests, so oxpeckers perform an important ecological service. Two species are known, both from Africa.

RED-BILLED OXPECKER
(Buphagus erythrorynchus)

The red-billed oxpecker makes a temporary home on rhinos, where it searches the folds of their thick skin looking for places where blood-sucking ticks gather. Some scientists think that, by allowing the oxpecker onto its back, the rhino takes advantage of the oxpecker's superior eyesight. If a red-billed oxpecker sees a predator in the distance, for instance, it lets out an alarm call that the rhino recognizes as meaning danger. For this reason, the red-billed oxpecker's Swahili name is *askari wa kifaru*, which means "the rhino's guard."

LENGTH: 20 cm

DIET: Ticks and mammal blood

FOUND IN: Savannas throughout sub-Saharan Africa

YELLOW-BILLED OXPECKER
(Buphagus africanus)

In a single day, a yellow-billed oxpecker can eat a hundred blood-sucking ticks and thousands of their babies. To gather extra energy, the yellow-billed oxpecker occasionally pecks at the host's skin to snack on blood.

As well as riding on large mammals like giraffes during the day, the yellow-billed oxpecker occasionally roosts on these animals at night. Flocks gather on the undersides of giraffes, for instance, nestling in the natural pockets that form at the top of each leg. This behavior keeps the yellow-billed oxpecker safe and warm. It is not known whether this causes the giraffe any distress.

LENGTH: 20 cm

DIET: Ticks and mammal blood

FOUND IN: Savannas throughout sub-Saharan Africa

PIGEONS AND DOVES

Seen commonly in towns and cities, pigeons and doves are intelligent, adaptable seed-eaters. Their nests are sometimes little more than flimsy platforms of sticks, arranged on trees, cliffs, and human buildings. Generally, pigeons are larger than doves, though the two words are often used loosely.

VICTORIA CROWNED PIGEON
(Goura victoria)

During the breeding season, the Victoria crowned pigeon becomes very territorial. Males regularly challenge one another to fights, which help individuals work out who it is best to avoid in the future. In these duels, individuals puff out their chests, raise their wings, and occasionally dash at one another at full pace.

Like many pigeons, the male Victoria crowned pigeon makes its wings clap loudly against one another when leaving its treetop perch. This show of strength is thought to attract the attention of nearby females.

LENGTH: 66–74 cm

FOUND IN: Swamp forests of northern New Guinea

DIET: Fallen fruits, seeds, and berries

THICK-BILLED GREEN PIGEON
(Treron curvirostra)

Skulking across the forest canopy, the thick-billed green pigeon searches for fig fruits to eat. Its broad beak helps the pigeon tear through the fruits' leathery skins. Occasionally, this pigeon gathers into small flocks that make brief visits to the forest floor to look for wild strawberries.

If startled by a predator, the thick-billed green pigeon can jump upward into the air and pump its wings with great power. This escape routine is especially effective in pigeons, which have larger, broader wings compared to other birds.

LENGTH: 22–31 cm

FOUND IN: Tropical forests across eastern parts of India and Southeast Asia

DIET: Fruits, especially figs

COMMON WOOD PIGEON
(Columba palumbus)

The untidy nest of the wood pigeon is often seen in trees in parks and gardens and sometimes near roads and train lines. Here, two hatchlings are tended to, regularly provided with "crop milk," which is a highly nutritious fluid produced in a pouch known as a crop at the back of the adult pigeon's throat.

Because they are relatively exposed, the common wood pigeon nest is often attacked by predators, especially crows. In urban areas, cats are another threat to chicks. Only about fifty per cent of wood pigeon babies live to see their first birthday.

LENGTH: 41–45 cm

DIET: Leaf buds, nuts, fruits, and berries

FOUND IN: Parks and gardens across Europe and Asia

ROCK DOVE
(Columba livia)

The rock dove is the world's most common wild bird. It has multiplied in towns and cities through a domesticated form known as the feral pigeon. The global success of the rock dove is down to its non-fussy diet and its preference for nesting in cliff-like places, especially tall buildings.

In many parts of the world, the rock dove can produce eggs throughout the year. This means that its numbers can rise quickly. When this happens, other city-dwelling animals, such as peregrine falcons, have plenty to eat.

LENGTH: 29–36 cm

DIET: Seeds, fruits, berries, and human scraps

FOUND IN: Towns and cities across the world

KINGFISHERS

These colorful birds live near ponds, streams, and rivers throughout Africa, Europe, and Asia and nest in special tunnels dug into the ground. In most species, the long, spear-like beak is used to catch fish and other water-dwelling animals.

COMMON KINGFISHER
(Alcedo atthis)

With its reflective blue feathers, the common kingfisher is one of the most eye-catching of all waterbirds. Yet it is also a fierce predator. Upon spotting a fish, it plunges into the water, sometimes diving 25 centimeters or more, and begins it underwater chase. Like many carnivorous birds, the bones in its meal are later vomited up in a tight, squashed-up pellet.

Unusually, the common kingfisher has no song. Instead, kingfishers impress one another with visual signals, like the bright blue feathers and orange beak.

LENGTH: 16–18 cm

FOUND IN: Slow-flowing streams, rivers, and lakes across Europe, Asia, and northern Africa

DIET: Fish and, less commonly, crustaceans, frogs, insects, and spiders

BROWN-HEADED PARADISE KINGFISHER
(Tanysiptera danae)

The brown-headed paradise kingfisher nests in termite mounds. When newly hatched, the chicks of the brown-headed paradise kingfisher are fed small beetles. As the chicks grow, the parents bring larger and larger menu items, including stick insects and praying mantises. This is unusual among kingfishers, who mostly eat fish.

The paradise kingfisher gets its name from its long, streamer-like tail feathers, which look like those of birds of paradise. These help males get noticed by females, who are attracted to individuals with the longest and boldest feathers.

LENGTH: 28–30 cm, including tail feathers

FOUND IN: Forests of southeastern New Guinea

DIET: Mostly insects, especially grasshoppers, beetles, and cicadas

BLACK-BACKED DWARF KINGFISHER
(Ceyx erithaca)

The black-backed dwarf kingfisher is one of the smallest of all kingfishers. Being small and nimble, this kingfisher can catch insects in flight and expertly peel spiders from their webs to eat. Larger prey, such as baby lizards, are killed by the kingfisher bashing them repeatedly against hard tree stumps and branches.

In pairs, the black-backed dwarf kingfisher creates nesting tunnels in stream banks, between tree roots, and even beside busy roads. This kingfisher can dig at a speed of almost 40 centimeters per hour.

LENGTH: 12–14 cm

DIET: Insects, spiders, and, occasionally, frogs and lizards

FOUND IN: Wetlands and forests across much of southern Asia

LAUGHING KOOKABURRA
(Dacelo novaeguineae)

This charismatic kingfisher is best known for its song: A manic-sounding cackle that can travel for miles across the Australian bush. These calls are usually performed by family groups who join in loudly with one another to signal to others nearby that the territory is taken and that rival kookaburras should stay away.

Being more stocky than other kingfishers, the laughing kookaburra is famous for eating larger prey, including venomous reptiles. This species has been known to eat snakes more than twice its own body length.

LENGTH: 39–42 cm

DIET: Varied, including mice, lizards, crustaceans, large insects, and snakes

FOUND IN: Forests and woodlands across eastern Australia

ROLLERS, MOTMOTS, AND BEE-EATERS

These colorful, insect-eating birds are distantly related to kingfishers. To prevent their insect prey from stinging or biting them, they repeatedly bash their catch against hard surfaces, such as rocks and tree trunks. Rollers, motmots, and bee-eaters are mostly found across Africa, Europe, and Asia, with the latter two living in long burrows.

LILAC-BREASTED ROLLER
(Coracias caudatus)

This bird is named after its unusual courtship dances, which look like an aerobatics display. In the breeding season, male and female rollers fly upward more than 100 meters into the sky before dropping to the ground, rolling as they fall. When near the ground, the pair swoop upward to repeat the process again. If rivals should approach during this display, the male lilac-breasted roller lets out a blast of raucous cawing and loud chuckling.

The lilac-breasted roller is incredibly defensive of its chicks, who it hides in crevices in tree trunks. When predators attack, such as snakes or crows, both parents attack the threat with sweeping glances of their wings, beak and claws. Even birds of prey, such as falcons, have been known to flee from the roller's fierce temper. Much of the lilac-breasted roller's life is spent perched on high objects, such as lightning-struck trees or telegraph posts, looking for animals below. In some parts of Africa, this roller sits near busy roads, watching for slow-moving lizards, chameleons, and snakes trying to cross from one side to the other.

LENGTH: 28–38 cm

DIET: Insects, spiders, small reptiles, and birds

FOUND IN: Open savannas across eastern and southern Africa

TRINIDAD MOTMOT
(Momotus bahamensis)

The Trinidad motmot is one of the most secretive birds in the world. Only a few times has its call, a haunting, owl-like hoot, been recorded. Like other motmots, it nests in underground burrows that can be up to 4 meters long.

As well as being used to show off to females, the long tail of the Trinidad motmot can be used as a way to communicate to predators. If a bird of prey flies overhead, the motmot rhythmically moves its tail right and left. This informs the predator that its stealthy approach has failed.

LENGTH: 46 cm

DIET: Insects and, occasionally, small reptiles

FOUND IN: Forests and woodlands of Trinidad and Tobago

EUROPEAN BEE-EATER
(Merops apiaster)

The male European bee-eater is devoted to its mate. After hunting, it gives large items of food, such as dragonflies, to the female and keeps for itself smaller food items, such as bees and wasps. Together, the male and female nest in a long burrow on a sandy cliff.

Bee-eaters wait until May before laying their eggs. This is when the number of insects in the environment begins to rise more sharply. It is said that, by the middle of summer, a European bee-eater can eat as many as 250 bees a day.

LENGTH: 25–29 cm

DIET: Insects, especially wasps, bees, and hornets

FOUND IN: Breeds in sloping meadows across scattered parts of Africa, Europe, and Asia

AUKS

Auks are seafaring waterbirds that are well-suited to diving into the water to chase fish. Propelled by their wings, some species can dive to depths of 180 meters or more. In total, there are twenty-five known auk species, including puffins, murres, and murrelets.

RAZOR-BILLED AUK
(Alca torda)

The razor-billed auk spends half of its life at sea, searching for schools of tiny fish that gather near the surface of the ocean. When it spots prey, it dives like a missile into the water and the chase begins. This auk can hold its breath while hunting for more than a minute.

When its belly is full, the razor-billed auk makes a journey of 10 kilometers or more back to its nesting colony to feed its young. Like many seabirds, the razor-billed auk mates with the same partner its whole life.

WINGSPAN: 63–68 cm

DIET: Baby fish, crustaceans, and sand-dwelling worms

FOUND IN: Rocky shores and cliffs throughout the northern Atlantic Ocean

THICK-BILLED MURRE
(Uria lomvia)

Weighing up to 1.5 kilograms, the thick-billed murre is the heaviest of all auks. It lives in busy breeding colonies, some containing one million or more birds. Packed together tightly in these noisy breeding grounds, the thick-billed murre has the smallest territory of any bird. It guards a plot just 30 centimeters by 30 centimeters in size.

Each individual murre has either a charismatic bill-stripe or an eye-stripe, but never both. These stripes help individuals recognize one another from a distance during the breeding season.

WINGSPAN: 63–68 cm

DIET: Baby fish, crustaceans, and sand-dwelling worms

FOUND IN: Rocky shores and cliffs throughout the northern Atlantic Ocean

ATLANTIC PUFFIN
(Fratercula arctica)

In a single dive, a puffin can catch as many as fifty small fish. Instead of swallowing its prey straight away, the puffin lines its catches up in its beak, holding them in place using a special tongue with lots of spiky grooves. The meal is taken back to feed its chick, hiding in a clifftop burrow on land.

Like many seabirds, puffins swallow lots of salty water while hunting. This salt is later squirted out from the body via special holes in the nostrils.

WINGSPAN: 47–63 cm

DIET: Fish, especially sand eels

FOUND IN: Remote coasts of northwestern Europe and eastern North America

JAPANESE MURRELET
(Synthliboramphus wumizusume)

With only a few thousand left in the wild, the Japanese murrelet is the rarest of all auks. Its recent disappearance is partly because its nests can be easily raided by rats and feral cats, who feed on their chicks. Because of predators like these, murrelet chicks grow very fast.

Within two days, Japanese murrelet chicks fledge the nest and take to the open sea, where they are taught to hunt by their parents. They stay together at sea by making a range of noisy, peeping flight calls.

WINGSPAN: 43 cm

DIET: Mostly crustaceans, including shrimp-like krill

FOUND IN: Remote coasts and rocky islands off mainland Japan

ALBATROSSES AND PETRELS

Never too far from the water, albatrosses and petrels are sometimes called "tubenoses" because of their tube-shaped nostrils. These are filled with extra blood vessels to help them smell food from far away. To save energy while traveling, tubenoses can lock their wing-bones into position when gliding.

WANDERING ALBATROSS
(Diomedea exulans)

With the largest wingspan in the world, the wandering albatross is one of Earth's most intrepid travelers. In a year, a single wandering albatross navigating the southern oceans can do a complete loop of the planet three times over—that's more than 120,000 kilometers.

During the breeding season, the wandering albatross returns to the same cliff-face each year to reunite with its breeding partner and lay a single egg. This egg is sat upon (incubated) for eleven weeks, longer than any other bird.

WINGSPAN: 250–350 cm

DIET: Squid, fish, and crustaceans

FOUND IN: Nests on remote islands in cooler parts of the southern hemisphere

BLACK-BROWED ALBATROSS
(Thalassarche melanophris)

Black-browed albatross colonies contain thousands of rowdy breeding pairs that make a lot of noise. Individuals bray and cackle angrily, seeking to protect their nests and alert one another to danger from hungry rats or predatory seabirds.

Like other albatrosses, black-browed albatross courtship takes years for hatchlings to learn. Adult males and females fan out their tail feathers, bow softly, and gently tap their beaks against one another, making a unique clacking sound.

WINGSPAN: 205–240 cm

DIET: Fish, crustaceans, and squid

FOUND IN: Nests on islands in the southern regions of the Atlantic and Pacific oceans

WILSON'S STORM PETREL
(Oceanites oceanicus)

About the same weight as a golf ball, Wilson's storm petrel is the smallest warm-blooded animal to breed in Antarctica.

Its lightweight body helps it catch tiny animals, known as zooplankton, floating near the surface of the water. Storm petrels grab their prey while hovering very close to the surface of the water and paddling their feet gently upon the crest of each wave—a technique called surface pattering. Others storm petrels like to surf the momentary gusts of wind that blow just over the surface of the water.

WINGSPAN: 34–42 cm

DIET: Zooplankton

FOUND IN: Nests on Antarctica and surrounding islands

SOUTHERN GIANT PETREL
(Macronectes giganteus)

Able to detect the smells of rotting seabirds and dead seals from kilometers away, the southern giant petrel is a spectacular scavenger. Yet this seabird is far more than a vulture of the seas. The southern giant petrel regularly attacks other animals, including young albatrosses, penguins and even humans.

Sailors used to call this tubenose the "stinkpot" for its nasty habit of descending upon and then pecking at sailors who had been knocked overboard.

WINGSPAN: 150–210 cm

DIET: Fish, squid, and carrion, including seals and whales

FOUND IN: Nests on islands throughout the southern oceans

CORMORANTS AND FRIGATEBIRDS

Cormorants and frigatebirds are part of a larger group of waterbirds known as Suliformes. Frigatebirds tend to live near tropical oceans, whereas cormorants are found near water all over the world. Their beaks are long and hooked at the tip to help grasp fish under the water.

DOUBLE-CRESTED CORMORANT
(Nannopterum auritum)

The double-crested cormorant fires through the water like a torpedo. Powered by its feet, its wings are used for steering toward its fish prey. It can hold its breath for up to 70 seconds and regularly dives to depths of more than 5 meters.

Like all cormorants, the double-crested cormorant is often seen standing next to water with its wings stretched out wide like a statue. Because cormorant feathers are not waterproof, like those of other waterbirds, this posture helps the cormorant dry its feathers out in the sun.

LENGTH: 70–90 cm

DIET: Fish and, occasionally, amphibians and crustaceans

FOUND IN: Wetlands and coastal regions across North America

RED-LEGGED CORMORANT
(Poikilocarbo gaimardi)

Streaked with feathers, seaweeds, and even bird droppings, the nest of the red-legged cormorant is placed as far away as possible from other cliff-dwelling seabirds. Like other cormorants, its chicks hatch early and are very dependent on their parents for protection. It can take ten weeks for chicks to grow enough to fledge the nest.

To blend in with its rocky surroundings, the red-legged cormorant has sleek, gray feathers. From a distance, only its colorful beak and feet are visible.

LENGTH: 71–76 cm

DIET: Fish, especially eels and anchovies

FOUND IN: Steep rockfaces on the eastern coast of South America and northern Australia

LITTLE PIED CORMORANT
(Microcarbo melanoleucos)

Being smaller than other cormorants, the little pied cormorant sometimes has trouble swallowing larger fish. Occasionally, this discomfort attracts other birds, particularly gulls, who attempt to steal its meal. This stealing behavior, which is especially common among waterbirds, is called kleptoparasitism.

Compared to other cormorants, the little pied cormorant is fond of crustaceans, including shrimps, which are found near the seafloor. In fresh waters, these small cormorants also eat the early life stages of water-dwelling insects, known as larvae or nymphs.

LENGTH: 55–65 cm

DIET: Fish, crustaceans, and young insects

FOUND IN: Swamps, lakes, lagoons, estuaries, and coastlines throughout Australasia

MAGNIFICENT FRIGATEBIRD
(Fregata magnificens)

The magnificent frigatebird is a well-known kleptoparasite. To steal food from other seabirds, it often harasses them, pecking at them again and again. This stress frequently causes the seabird to vomit up its meal, which the frigatebird quickly devours.

Occasionally, the magnificent frigatebird hunts for itself. By gliding just above the surface of the water, frigatebirds can catch flying fish as they leap from the water. As with cormorants, frigatebirds lack waterproof feathers.

LENGTH: 89–114 cm

DIET: Stolen foods from other birds, as well as squid and flying fish

FOUND IN: Tropical Atlantic and Pacific coastlines and islands

CRANES

Cranes live in grasslands and wetlands across most continents. With fifteen species in total, the group includes some of the world's tallest flying birds. Unlike many long-necked birds, cranes hold the head horizontally in front of the body when flying.

GRAY CROWNED CRANE
(Balearica regulorum)

During the day, the gray crowned crane hunts by stomping its long feet through the undergrowth, catching startled prey as it tries to escape. These cranes also like to stand near large animals, such antelopes and gazelle, whose lumbering movement through the grasslands flushes out other animals to eat.

With long, backward-pointing toes that help it to grasp branches, the gray crowned crane is one of the only cranes able to sleep in trees.

HEIGHT: 100–110 cm

DIET: Seeds, plants, worms, insects, frogs, fish, and snakes

FOUND IN: Marshes, grasslands, and dry savannas throughout sub-Saharan Africa

RED-CROWNED CRANE
(Grus japonensis)

With its sensitive beak, the red-crowned crane can feel for animals or plants in murky waters. Should a startled fish make a sudden escape, the red-crowned crane flexes its neck forward in a stabbing motion. To break its prey into bite-size chunks, the red-crowned crane holds its meal firmly in its beak and shakes it vigorously.

The bold colors of this crane and its graceful charisma are celebrated by many East Asian societies, who see it as a symbol of luck, long life, and loyalty.

HEIGHT: 150–158 cm

DIET: Fish, amphibians, crustaceans, and some wetland plants

FOUND IN: Mudflats, wetlands, marshes, and rivers of East Asia

SARUS CRANE
(Antigone antigone)

The sarus crane is the tallest flying bird in the world. At 1.8 meters, it stands taller than the average human. Unlike many cranes, the sarus crane rarely makes long seasonal journeys (known as migrations) between winter and summer grounds. Instead, pairs spend the year defending a territory around a single nest made from piled-up reeds.

Like other cranes, sarus crane pairs form long-lasting bonds which are renewed each year through loud trumpeting and a leaping, ballet-like dance.

HEIGHT: 180 cm

DIET: Wetland plants, fish, frogs, crustaceans, and insects

FOUND IN: Wetlands and grasslands throughout South Asia, Southeast Asia, and Australasia

DEMOISELLE CRANE
(Anthropoides virgo)

The smallest of all cranes endures the toughest of migrations. At the end of each summer, individuals throughout Asia gather in large flocks of 400 or more and prepare to make their journey south to India. Flying at an altitude of more than 7,000 meters, the demoiselle crane navigates its way through the Himalayan mountains, avoiding starvation and predatory golden eagles along the way.

In its wintering grounds, demoiselle cranes are known to form super-flocks with other cranes. Sometimes these flocks contain 20,000 or more cranes.

HEIGHT: 90–100 cm

DIET: Plants and their seeds, insects, and small mammals

FOUND IN: Breeds in grasslands and semi-deserts throughout Europe and Asia

DUCKS

Generally, ducks have shorter necks and smaller bodies than geese and swans, their close relatives. Like others in this group, ducks have a beak with tiny, tooth-like bumps across its outer edges.

MALLARD
(Anas platyrhynchos)

Sleeping with one eye open, the mallard remains watchful for larger animals, especially at night. Its predators include foxes, cats, weasels, and even snakes. In North America alone, mallards are hunted by fifteen different birds of prey. To steer clear of threats like these, mallard chicks hatch fully formed and are ready to swim within minutes of hatching.

In the weeks that follow, the chicks stay close to their mother, learning which foods are safe and which are to be avoided.

LENGTH: 50–65 cm

DIET: Water plants, insects, crustaceans, and fish

FOUND IN: Wetlands throughout the world

COMMON EIDER
(Somateria mollissima)

Flying at more than 70 miles an hour, the common eider is both the fastest and heaviest of all wild ducks. It cruises across coastal waters in vast flocks, sometimes numbering 100 or more individuals.

The common eider is best known for the soft feathers on its underside, which were once collected by humans to make comfy pillows. Nesting eiders pluck these feathers from the chest and use them to make a soft lining for the nest. Common eiders regularly nest close to their brothers and sisters—they even babysit one another's chicks.

LENGTH: 50–71 cm

DIET: Crabs and shellfish, especially mussels

FOUND IN: Nests in colonies along rocky coasts, often on islands

MANDARIN DUCK
(Aix galericulata)

Unlike most ducks, the mandarin duck lays its eggs in trees. In spring, when its clutch of up to twelve eggs hatches, the female flies to the ground. From there, she encourages the ducklings to make a "leap of faith" down to the ground.

Like many ducks, the mandarin duck spends much of its day "dabbling"—tipping its body downward into the water to reach for aquatic plants or swimming insect larvae below.

LENGTH: 41–51 cm

DIET: Plants, seeds, and small animals, including snails and insects

FOUND IN: Once widespread across East Asia, this species has now been introduced to many other parts of the world

MADAGASCAR POCHARD
(Aythya innotata)

Many years ago, the Madagascar pochard was feared to be extinct. This was partly because its wetland habitats were removed to make way for rice fields. Then, in 2006, a small group of these secretive ducks was discovered living in a volcanic lake in a remote part of Madagascar.

Like many types of pochard, the Madagascar pochard spends forty per cent or more of its day feeding. It dives again and again into the depths, hunting for aquatic insects that mostly live on the lake floor.

LENGTH: 45–56 cm

DIET: Aquatic insects

FOUND IN: Remote lakes in Madagascar and the Comoro Islands

FLAMINGOS

These eye-catching waterbirds feed by sieving food from out of the water using a specialized beak. Their pink color comes from chemicals contained within their diet of tiny animals and plants. In total, six species have been discovered.

GREATER FLAMINGO
(Phoenicopterus roseus)

The greater flamingo is a natural make-up artist. By combing special oils produced near the tail into its feathers, the greater flamingo can make itself a more vibrant pink. This comes in handy during the breeding season, when flamingos need to look their best.

Like all flamingos, the greater flamingo uses its long toes to kick up mud under the water. It then runs its long, sieve-like beak through the cloudy water to gather food.

LENGTH: 120–125 cm

DIET: Plankton

FOUND IN: Wetlands from northern Africa throughout the Middle East and into southern and central Europe

LESSER FLAMINGO
(Phoeniconaias minor)

Big cats, hyenas, eagles, and foxes are just some of the predators who regularly eat the lesser flamingo. To guard against these threats, young flamingos gather together in groups known as creches, sometimes 100,000 or more in size, which are watched over by adults.

Because the habitats of the greater flamingo and the lesser flamingo sometimes overlap, the two species are regularly mistaken for one another. The lesser flamingo has a darker beak.

LENGTH: 80–90 cm

DIET: Plankton, particularly the algae known as *Spirulina*

FOUND IN: Wetlands of sub-Saharan Africa and western India

CHILEAN FLAMINGO
(Phoenicopterus chilensis)

By wagging its head from side to side and saluting with its wings, the Chilean flamingo does all it can to grab the attention of its mate. Together, males and females build a pillar-like nest out of mud. On it, they lay a single egg, which they then take turns to incubate.

Young flamingos take up to four years to grow. To help them put on weight, adults provide their young with a special fluid produced deep within the throat known as crop milk. This pink goo is highly nutritious.

LENGTH: 100–110 cm

DIET: Plankton

FOUND IN: Coastal mudflats, estuaries, lagoons, and salt lakes throughout central and southern South America

AMERICAN FLAMINGO
(Phoenicopterus ruber)

Because its feathers are more blushed than those of other flamingos, this species is sometimes called the rosy flamingo. It was once common in parts of the USA, forming great flocks of 2,000 or more birds.

Like all flamingos, the American flamingo spends much of its time resting on one leg. Why flamingos stand like this remains a mystery, although some scientists think that the behavior may help reduce the amount of body heat lost through the feet.

LENGTH: 120–145 cm

DIET: Plankton

FOUND IN: Breeds in wetlands across Central America, Colombia, Venezuela, and northern Brazil, as well as parts of the Caribbean

GANNETS AND BOOBIES

These diving waterbirds, known as sulids, are closely related to one another. Their bodies are long and streamlined like an arrow. This shape helps when hunting for fish, as the bird's body can effortlessly pierce the surface of the water.

NORTHERN GANNET
(Morus bassanus)

Hitting the water at speeds of up to 60 miles per hour, the northern gannet travels more than 10 meters into the water in search of fish and squid. Its large, forward-facing eyes provide binocular vision, helping the gannet keep track of prey underwater. Food is swallowed whole, before the gannet returns to the sky.

Gannets are noisy, sociable birds that nest very close to one another on cliffs. Unlike other birds, which use special downy feathers on the underside of the body to help incubate their eggs, the northern gannet uses its feet. Blood gathers in its webbed toes, causing the feet to heat up like a hot water bottle.

Gannet hatchlings begin feeding quickly. By reaching their beaks into the open mouth of their mother or father, the chicks encourage their parents to vomit up half-digested fish that they swallow greedily. Unlike other chicks, northern gannet hatchlings rarely move around their nests or flap their wings. This reduces the chance that they might accidentally fall out of the nest.

LENGTH: 93–110 cm

DIET: Fish and squid

FOUND IN: Cliffs and remote, rocky islands on both sides of the Atlantic Ocean

MASKED BOOBY
(Sula dactylatra)

After spotting prey, the masked booby can dive from a height of 100 meters into the water. Special sacs of air hidden beneath the surface of the skin on its head cushion the impact generated when it collides with the water's surface.

The name "booby" was probably a mistranslation of the Spanish word *bobo*, which means "stupid." This is because, many years ago, these birds had a habit of landing on sailing ships, where they were promptly captured and eaten by sailors.

LENGTH: 74–86 cm

DIET: Fish, especially flying fish

FOUND IN: Coastlines and coastal waters in tropical oceans across the world

BLUE-FOOTED BOOBY
(Sula nebouxii)

Waving its bright blue feet and strutting confidently up and down the rockface, the male blue-footed booby is hard to miss. These dances allow females to work out who the healthiest individual to mate with is, and who might provide most for the hatchlings.

Males and females of this booby species have different approaches to hunting. Females tend to dive deep, sometimes up to 20 meters, whereas males stick nearer to the surface. Some scientists think this could be a way for parents to catch a wider variety of food for their chicks.

LENGTH: 81–86 cm

DIET: Fish

FOUND IN: The eastern Pacific Ocean, from the USA to Peru and the Galápagos Islands

GEESE AND SWANS

Along with ducks, geese and swans form a large group of water-dwelling birds known as the Anatidae. Geese and swans have long and flexible necks, which they use to reach for water-plants or smaller animals swimming underwater. Their distinct calls include honks, quacks, and trumpeting sounds.

BAR-HEADED GOOSE
(Anser indicus)

The bar-headed goose is a record-breaking high-flier. When this species migrates over the Himalayan mountains, individuals can reach altitudes of more than 7,000 meters. There is even a claim of one being heard flying over Mount Everest, almost 9,000 meters high.

Flying high like this is hard for birds, because there is less oxygen at altitude to power its wingbeats. For this reason, the bar-headed goose has evolved blood that can more readily carry oxygen around the body and a heart better equipped for pumping.

LENGTH: 71–76 cm

DIET: Grasses, roots, stems, and leaves

FOUND IN: Central Asia in summer and South Asia in winter

CANADA GOOSE
(Branta canadensis)

On its seasonal migrations across North America, the Canada goose frequently flies in an energy-saving V-formation across the sky. The geese at the front stir the air up as they move through it, swirling it upward so that the geese at the back become momentarily lifted. To stop the frontmost goose getting tired, Canada geese regularly swap their positions in the formation.

In modern times, the Canada goose strays far from its North American homeland. Released by humans, the species has established itself in thousands of parks and cities around the world.

LENGTH: 90–115 cm

FOUND IN: Worldwide

DIET: Grasses, roots, stems, and leaves

MUTE SWAN
(Cygnus olor)

The mute swan is far from quiet. Grunting, snorting, and hissing, especially to scare away predators, are just some of its calls. When flying, the mute swan's wings also make a loud throbbing sound that can be heard from up to a mile away. This whirring sound helps family groups keep close to one another in mist and clouds.

Unlike ducks and geese, male and female mute swans build their nest together. Made of sticks and pondweeds, these nesting platforms can be more than 3 meters across and are weatherproof enough to be used again and again.

LENGTH: 127–152 cm

FOUND IN: Wetlands across Europe, Asia, and northern Africa

DIET: Waterweeds and crop plants, including wheat

BLACK SWAN
(Cygnus atratus)

Like all swans, the black swan is fiercely protective. Should a predator show an interest in its chicks, the male and female chase them away angrily, waving their powerful wings while hissing and snapping. The black swan has even been known to attack humans.

For nine months the pair look after their young, known as cygnets. Sometimes, to keep extra-safe, cygnets ride upon their mother's back, nestled beneath her closed wings.

LENGTH: 110–140 cm

DIET: Waterweeds and algae

FOUND IN: Wetlands of southwestern and southeastern Australia

GREBES AND LOONS

These fast and nimble waterbirds use their flippers to power after prey. Because they share the same swimming technique, scientists once thought that these two groups were related to one another, but recent discoveries show they come from different branches of the bird family tree.

GREAT CRESTED GREBE
(Podiceps cristatus)

The courtship dance of the great crested grebe is celebrated among birdwatchers. In water, the male and female press their chests together and rhythmically pump their wings so that they appear to rise out of the water. To show off their nesting skills while courting, these grebes sometimes fill their beaks with waterweeds.

The great crested grebe nest contains four chicks that can swim very soon after hatching. To improve their swimming skills, the parent grebe carries its young on its back and then starts to dive, encouraging them deeper into the water.

LENGTH: 46–61 cm

DIET: Fish and crustaceans

FOUND IN: Lakes throughout Europe and Asia and parts of Australasia and Africa

AUSTRALASIAN GREBE
(Tachybaptus novaehollandiae)

The Australasian grebe is a master escape artist. If threatened by a predator, such as a hawk or a large snake, this small grebe dives down, swims secretively away underwater, and resurfaces far from the gaze of its attacker.

To keep extra-dry, the Australasian grebe has 20,000 closely packed feathers to provide it with insulation. It has more than four times the number of feathers that many other birds possess.

LENGTH: 23–27 cm

DIET: Fish, crustaceans, and snails

FOUND IN: Fresh waters throughout Australia, New Zealand, and nearby Pacific islands

ARCTIC LOON
(Gavia arctica)

The Arctic loon is one of the deadliest of all seabirds. When hunting, four out of five of its dives result in a catch. This impressive hit-rate is down to its sharp eyes, arrow-like beak, and preference for hunting in lakes with especially clear water. The Arctic loon rarely strays from sunlit surface waters.

The oval-shaped nest of the Arctic loon is often found within a meter of the water's edge. Exposed to predators like foxes and weasels, parent birds remain highly protective of their young.

LENGTH: 58–73 cm

DIET: Fish and, less commonly, insects, shellfish, and waterweeds

FOUND IN: Lakes in cold, northern regions of Europe, Asia, and Alaska

COMMON LOON
(Gavia immer)

The common loon walks clumsily on land but in the water, using its powerful flippers, it can swim twice as fast as an Olympic swimmer. Unlike many seabirds, the common loon is a deep diver. Some individuals have been known to dive 70 meters or more. With a single breath, the common loon can spend a minute underwater.

Mostly, the loon swallows fish whole in the water. To help grind the food up, loons—like many birds—regularly swallow pebbles to sit in the stomach. These are known as gastroliths.

LENGTH: 66–91 cm

DIET: Mostly fish

FOUND IN: Lakes in northern regions, including North America, Iceland, and Norway

GULLS, TERNS, AND SKIMMERS

These noisy seabirds, known as larids, eat a wide variety of food. In the case of some gulls, this includes human garbage. They spend much of their time in the air, scanning the land below for things to eat. Worldwide, 100 species have been discovered and named.

GREAT BLACK-BACKED GULL
(Larus marinus)

With a large wingspan similar to that of some eagles, the great black-backed gull is the largest of all larids. It doesn't have large claws or the eagle's hooked beak, and so it relies on relentless aggression and brute force to overpower its prey.

The bulky body of the great black-backed gull is maintained partly by eating human garbage. Fifty per cent of its meals come, in some way, from human waste. Only when feeding its chicks does the gull focus on its traditional diet of fish.

LENGTH: 71–79 cm

DIET: Fish, squid, crustaceans, starfish, and human garbage

FOUND IN: Northern Atlantic ocean and waters off northern Scandinavia and Russia

BLACK SKIMMER
(Rynchops niger)

With a unique beak that looks like an open pair of scissors, the black skimmer flies powerfully just above the surface of the water. As it moves, it lets its lower beak skim through the water. Here, the sensitive beak "feels" for the vibrations of fish trying to get out of the way.

Skimmers are the only birds in the world to have evolved slit-shaped pupils, like those of some snakes. This adaptation helps them spot prey moving at high speeds close to the beak.

LENGTH: 40–50 cm

DIET: Small fish, insects, and crustaceans

FOUND IN: Rivers, coasts, and wetlands across South America and southern USA

ARCTIC TERN
(Sterna paradisaea)

The Arctic tern makes by far the longest migration of any animal on Earth. Each year it makes a journey of 44,000 miles, going all the way from the Arctic to Antarctica, and back again. In a single lifetime, often thirty years or more, this tern can rack up more than 15 million miles, which is the equivalent of traveling to the moon and back three times.

By migrating long distances, the Arctic tern chases the warmest seasons across the globe, from north to south and back again. This means that it never has to endure the long nights of winter, when finding food becomes difficult. To save energy while traveling, the Arctic tern makes use of naturally occurring wind patterns that direct it over useful feeding and resting grounds, as if on a conveyor belt.

Like all terns, the wings of the Arctic tern are long and thin and its head is shaped like an arrow. This makes terns very streamlined, helping them slice through the water surface while chasing fish.

LENGTH: 28–39 cm

DIET: Fish

FOUND IN: Breeds off the coasts of Arctic regions

HERONS AND ALLIES

Herons and their "allies," the ibises, bitterns, and spoonbills, are large waterbirds with long necks and sharp beaks. They are known for their four long toes and a special toenail-like claw on each foot used for grooming feathers. The group is closely related to pelicans and shoebills, forming a bigger group known as the Pelecaniformes.

BLACK HERON
(Egretta ardesiaca)

By gathering its wings around its head, the black heron creates a sunshade over the water where secretive fish gather to seek shelter from the sun. Into this shade, the black heron uses its long, pointed beak to stab at unsuspecting fish too slow to escape.

Like all herons, the black heron regularly gathers in large groups, sometimes up to 100 or more in number. To protect itself from predators at night, the black heron sleeps alongside others in these flocks. This behavior, performed by many birds, is known as roosting.

LENGTH: 43–66 cm

DIET: Fish

FOUND IN: Lakes, rivers, ponds, and some coastal areas across much of Africa

AFRICAN SACRED IBIS
(Threskiornis aethiopicus)

With its long and curved beak, the African sacred ibis can reach prey other birds struggle to reach. As well as plucking maggots from dead animals, caterpillars from leaves and beetle grubs from tree trunks, this species is also known to raid the nests of other animals, including crocodiles.

The African sacred ibis was once treated as a god by ancient Egyptian civilisations. Thousands of years ago, millions of these birds were mummified and entombed in special burial ceremonies.

LENGTH: 65–89 cm

DIET: Plants and animals. Occasionally visits garbage heaps

FOUND IN: Wetlands and mudflats, especially in sub-Saharan Africa

GREAT BITTERN
(Botaurus stellaris)

On a calm night, the great bittern's foghorn call can be heard from almost 5 kilometers away. To produce this booming song, the bittern sucks in lots of air and then blasts it out all at once, using its oesophagus (food pipe) as an echo chamber.

The great bittern is a master of camouflage. When spooked by a predator, this secretive waterbird lifts its head to the sky and stands statue-still. When it does this, the stripy brown feathers on the throat perfectly match the reedbeds in which it lives, making it seem to disappear into its surroundings.

LENGTH: 64–80 cm

DIET: Fish, amphibians, and large insects

FOUND IN: Reedbeds across cooler regions of Europe and Asia

ROSEATE SPOONBILL
(Platalea ajaja)

By gently moving its sensitive beak left and right through the water, the spoonbill feels for fish trying to make an escape. It eats other animals too, including small snails and crustaceans. By eating lots of different prey, the roseate spoonbill can live alongside other wetland birds without competing with them for food.

More than a century ago, this species was almost hunted to extinction for its charismatic pink feathers, which were once used to decorate hats and clothing.

LENGTH: 71–86 cm

DIET: Small fish, insects, snails, and crustaceans

FOUND IN: Wetlands and shallow coastal waters throughout South America, the Caribbean, and southern USA

PELICANS AND SHOEBILLS

These closely related groups of waterbirds have stocky beaks used to catch fish and four webbed toes on each foot. One of the toes has a comb-like edge used to brush feathers. Mostly, these birds eat fish, which they swallow whole. They include some of the largest birds in the world.

DALMATIAN PELICAN
(Pelecanus crispus)

With a body almost as heavy as a swan and a wingspan comparable to some albatrosses, the Dalmatian pelican is the largest of all pelicans. It nests in noisy social groups that sometimes contain more than 100 individuals. Watchful eyes guard the eggs from nest thieves, which include jackals and wolves.

Like all pelicans, a pouch under the beak can be used to carry and store food temporarily. In addition, when the weather is hot, the Dalmatian pelican can spread out the skin on its pouch to get rid of body heat more quickly, cooling it down.

LENGTH: 160–180 cm

DIET: Mainly fish

FOUND IN: Lakes, rivers, estuaries, and wetlands across Europe and Asia

AUSTRALIAN PELICAN
(Pelecanus conspicillatus)

The Australian pelican rarely hunts alone. These pelicans paddle together in large groups in shallow waters, forcing schools of fish closer and closer to the shore. Using their sensitive beaks to feel for prey underwater, hundreds of fish can be eaten at a time.

Occasionally, the Australian pelican targets larger animals, including pigeons and ducks. There are even rare reports of Australian pelicans attacking and eating one another, especially fledglings—a rare case of animal cannibalism.

LENGTH: 150–190 m

DIET: Fish, crustaceans, birds, small reptiles, amphibians, and mammals

FOUND IN: Open wetlands across Australia and Tasmania

SHOEBILL
(Balaeniceps rex)

The shoebill is named after its enormous, shoe-shaped beak. As with pelicans, the beak is triangular when looked at from the front, but the shoebill has a nail-like edge at the end of the beak used for pulling prey apart.

With long, splayed-out toes, the shoebill can stand upon floating rafts of waterweeds and wait for fish to surface nearby. Scientists think that the shoebill is especially fond of hippopotamuses. As these large animals swim past underwater, terrified fish escape to the surface, straight toward the shoebill's open beak.

LENGTH: 120 cm

DIET: Fish, birds, and, occasionally, baby crocodiles

FOUND IN: Tropical freshwater swamps across Central Africa

PERUVIAN PELICAN
(Pelecanus thagus)

When hunting, the Peruvian pelican plunges into the water like a spear. From a shallow height, it drops downward upon fish, striking out with a sturdy beak as long as a child's arm. Special air bubbles in its bones mean that, when submerged in the water, it quickly bobs back up to the surface.

Unusually for pelicans, the Peruvian pelican can also hunt at night. At sunset, individuals fly out to sea to search for schools of anchovies. At dawn the following day, their stomachs full, the Peruvian pelicans return to shore.

LENGTH: 140–150 cm

DIET: Mostly fish, especially anchovies

FOUND IN: Shallow coastal waters on the western coast of South America

PENGUINS

With a long, missile-shaped body and powerful flippers, penguins are the most specialized of all fish-hunting birds. Nearly all species are found in the southern hemisphere, where they spend about half of their time hunting at sea and the other half resting or caring for their young on land.

EMPEROR PENGUIN
(Aptenodytes forsteri)

The emperor penguin is the deepest diver of all birds. In pursuit of fish and squid, it has been known to dive to depths of 500 meters or more on a single breath. To stay submerged for longer, its organs can temporarily switch off to reduce the body's need for oxygen. Some dives can last twenty minutes.

On land, the emperor penguin is an impressive walker. Each year, in winter, individuals make an epic 100-kilometer journey across frozen Antarctica to nursery grounds. This is the only bird on the planet that can survive at the South Pole.

LENGTH: 112–115 cm

DIET: Fish and squid

FOUND IN: Waters off Antarctica

KING PENGUIN
(Aptenodytes patagonicus)

When chasing fish and squid, the king penguin can swim almost twice the speed of an Olympic swimmer. Mostly, this penguin stays submerged for five minutes at a time, but sometimes, when chasing shoals of fish, the king penguin jumps in and out of the water, taking a fresh breath each time it surfaces as if it were a dolphin.

Like other penguins, on land the king penguin walks with a waddling manner. But the king penguin can also move on land by "tobogganing"—sliding forward on its belly, powered by its feet and flippers.

LENGTH: 94–95 cm

DIET: Fish and squid

FOUND IN: Islands between Antarctica and the southern tip of South America

ROYAL PENGUIN
(Eudyptes schlegeli)

Royal penguin colonies are noisy and crowded. Trumpeting and donkey-like calls fill the air as parents return from hunting at sea and attempt to find their breeding partner or nestlings. Like many seabirds, adults regurgitate fish directly into the mouths of their young.

When royal penguin chicks reach one month in age, they are kept together in special nursery groups known as creches. Here, they are watched over by adults, who protect them from predatory birds including skuas and giant petrels.

LENGTH: 73–76 cm

DIET: Fish and squid

FOUND IN: Coasts of Macquarie Island, between Antarctica and New Zealand

LITTLE PENGUIN
(Eudyptula minor)

As the name suggests, the little penguin is small—about as tall as a cat. Unlike larger penguins, the little penguin nests in a sandy burrow lined with grasses and leaves. It has even been encouraged to nest in specially made nest-boxes put in place by humans.

In its nest, the little penguin spends much of its time cleaning its feathers. As with other penguins, the little penguin smears its feathers with drops of oil collected from a special gland hidden near the tail. This oil helps keep the feathers waterproof and streamlined while the bird is swimming.

LENGTH: 40–45 cm

DIET: Fish, squid, and, occasionally, crustaceans

FOUND IN: Breeds on isolated coasts of southern Australia and New Zealand

RAILS, FINFOOTS, AND LIMPKINS

Along with cranes, these waterbirds form a group known as the Gruiformes. With long necks, slender bodies, and sharp, pointed bills, these birds are important wetland predators, keeping numbers of shrimps and freshwater snails in check. Many species make a startling alarm call that sounds like a wail or a scream.

DUSKY MOORHEN
(Gallinula tenebrosa)

Seeds, grasses, algae, fruits, snails, bird droppings, and dead animals are just some of the things that the dusky moorhen is known to eat. Its non-fussy diet means that it can live alongside other wetland birds without competing with them for food.

During the breeding season, to tell rivals it is alert and, if required, ready to fight, the dusky moorhen wags its black and white tail back and forth. It bellows out a loud "KRIK" call, which can be heard more than a mile away, to mark its territory.

LENGTH: 35–40 cm

DIET: A wide range of plants, algae, and animals

FOUND IN: Wetlands across India, Australia, New Guinea, Borneo, and Indonesia

GUAM RAIL
(Hypotaenidia owstoni)

The Guam rail has come back from the very brink of extinction. In the late 1980s, numbers of rails went down so swiftly that the remaining handful were removed from Guam, their island home, and rehomed in zoos, where attempts to get them to breed were successful.

This rail's numbers plummeted because, after World War II, some tree snakes were accidentally released on its island. These snakes reproduced quickly and began eating the Guam rail and its eggs. Accidental releases of predators onto islands is one of the leading causes of bird extinctions around the world.

LENGTH: 28 cm

DIET: Snails, slugs, insects, and lizards, as well as leaves

FOUND IN: Now found on Cocos Island and Rota Island

LIMPKIN
(Aramus guarauna)

With its loud, wailing call, often performed at night, the limpkin is sometimes called the "crying bird." Its eerie song has been used as a spooky sound effect in many films, including *Tarzan* and films in the Harry Potter franchise.

The call, produced by the male limpkin, keeps rival males off its turf. Limpkin territories can be very large, occupying a space that is the same as eight football fields linked together. As long as there is enough food, these territories are guarded by both males and females all year around.

LENGTH: 63–73 cm

DIET: Mostly snails

FOUND IN: Wetlands across much of Central and South America and southern parts of the USA

AFRICAN FINFOOT
(Podica senegalensis)

Secretive and shy, the African finfoot stands statue-still at the water's edge. Its nest is constructed from little more than a few twigs and some reeds placed on fallen branches overhanging water.

When hunting, this species pays close attention to passing crocodiles and swimming buffaloes, who stir up the mud on the bottom of rivers and streams. Within this mist of mud can sometimes be found water-dwelling insects, which the African finfoot greedily snaps up.

LENGTH: 35–59 cm

DIET: Invertebrates, especially insects, spiders, millipedes, shrimps, and snails

FOUND IN: Rivers, streams, and lakes across Africa

STORKS

Storks tend to live in drier habitats than their close relatives, the herons and ibises. Their long, stout beaks are used for striking at prey, which includes fish, frogs, salamanders, snakes, lizards, and small mammals. Unlike other large birds, storks often communicate by loudly clacking their beaks.

WHITE STORK
(Ciconia ciconia)

The white stork is an impressive tool-user. Using its beak, the adult stork finds a large clump of moss and soaks it in a lake or river. Once it is full of water, like a sponge, the adult carries the wet moss back to the nest to provide a cool drink for its hatchlings.

Often, white storks use human buildings as places to construct their large, table-sized nests. The spires of churches are especially favored. The presence of white storks, returning to a nest year on year, is considered a good omen by many.

LENGTH: 100–102 cm

DIET: Worms, insects, amphibians, reptiles, and small mammals

FOUND IN: Meadows throughout Europe, northern Africa, and western Asia

JABIRU
(Jabiru mycteria)

Standing almost as high as a human adult, the jabiru is the tallest flying bird in South America. The jabiru dips its beak, held slightly open, into the water, where it feels for fish and other animals. If prey is detected, the beak is slammed shut and the meal swallowed whole. The jabiru's beak is as long as a human forearm.

In a local South American dialect, *jabiru* means "swollen neck." Its large, stretchy neck pouch can be used in the breeding season to show off to potential love-matches.

LENGTH: 122–140 cm

DIET: Insects, fish, frogs, snakes, and, occasionally, young caiman crocodiles

FOUND IN: Woodlands, gardens, and urban areas of South America

MARABOU STORK
(Leptoptilos crumenifer)

The marabou stork regularly socializes with vultures. It lets the vultures tear up dead animals first and then, when they are full, it steps up to finish the meal. Just like with vultures, the marabou stork has a bald head that can easily be cleaned after being poked into dead animals.

The scavenging lifestyle of the marabou stork has seen it become common around large trash heaps in Africa. As well as eating food waste, some marabou storks have been known to eat other items, including shoes and scraps of metal.

LENGTH: 115–152 cm

FOUND IN: Swamps, grasslands, and savannas throughout Africa

DIET: Carrion and human waste

WHITE-BELLIED STORK
(Ciconia abdimii)

When grasslands are struck by wildfires, the white-bellied stork makes an appearance. These storks walk in front of the flames, picking off large insects trying to make an escape. When fires are especially widespread, great flocks of white-bellied storks can gather, sometimes hunting alongside larger species of stork.

The white-bellied stork is fond of catching grasshoppers, especially locusts. Farmers appreciate the white-bellied stork for its hunting skills, since locusts are one of the biggest threats to farming in many parts of Africa.

LENGTH: 75–81 cm

FOUND IN: Grasslands and savannas throughout Africa

DIET: Mostly large insects

WADERS

Closely related to auks and gulls, waders are a group of wetland birds often seen walking through mudflats and shorelines looking for food buried in sand or mud. Their beaks differ dramatically according to the types of prey they eat. In North America these birds are often known as shorebirds.

WESTERN SANDPIPER
(Calidris mauri)

The western sandpiper is the most common wader in the world. Each spring, millions of these waders fly north as ice starts to melt on the snowy tundra near the Arctic circle. In the wet tundra soil, the western sandpiper probes for worms and small crustaceans, as well as spiders and insects.

To provide an energy boost during its migration, the western sandpiper regularly feeds upon a thin layer of green goo that gathers on wet mud. Known as biofilm, this slimy snack is slurped up using a tongue covered in lots of tiny bristles.

LENGTH: 14–17 cm

DIET: Insects, spiders, crustaceans, snails, and worms

FOUND IN: Breeds in tundra throughout eastern Siberia and Alaska

SOCIABLE LAPWING
(Vanellus gregarius)

In great flocks, sometimes 8,000 strong, the sociable lapwing travels across the Middle East to its wintering grounds in Asia. Unlike other waders, the sociable lapwing prefers dry grasslands to wetlands.

The sociable lapwing's nest is, like those of many waders, very simple. Lapwings simply scrape a hole in the ground, no larger or deeper than a dinner plate, and fill it with leaves, twigs, and small pebbles. Its eggs are often attacked by predators, especially rooks and crows. Another threat is cows, who occasionally step on lapwing nests by accident.

LENGTH: 27–30 cm

DIET: Spiders and insects, especially grasshoppers, beetles, and caterpillars

FOUND IN: Breeds in dry grasslands of Kazakhstan

RUFF
(Calidris pugnax)

This wader is named for the male's decorated tufts of feathers on its neck, which look like a "ruff"—a disk-shaped fashion accessory worn in medieval times. In spring, male ruffs gather at special proving grounds, known as leks, to show off their unusual neck-ware.

Not all males develop a ruff. Some have brown feathers like female birds. These males, known as faeders, walk among the females as they gather at leks. Sometimes, while the other males are preoccupied with displaying, it is the faeders that are given the opportunity to breed with females.

LENGTH: 20–32 cm

FOUND IN: Breeds in wetlands in colder regions of northern Europe and Asia

DIET: Mostly water-dwelling insects and their larvae

BUSH STONE-CURLEW
(Burhinus grallarius)

On moonlit nights, the bush stone-curlew walks upon long legs through the undergrowth. Its large eyes are sensitive to moving prey, which it snaps up with a dagger-like beak. Once its stomach is full, the bush stone-curlew returns to tall grasses to rest.

To avoid predators during the day, the bush stone-curlew stands like a statue. Sometimes the sudden appearance of a rival wader can also cause the bush stone-curlew to freeze. Bush stone-curlews have been known to stand still for hours in front of shop windows, where they mistake their reflection for a rival bird.

LENGTH: 54–59 cm

FOUND IN: Grasslands across Australia

DIET: Mostly insects, with some small amphibians, mammals, and reptiles

KAGUS AND SUNBITTERNS

Though they look different, these two strange ground-dwelling birds are related to one another. Not all scientists agree about where they should be placed in the bird family tree, but it is likely that they are part of a larger group of birds that were once numerous but have since faced extinction.

KAGU
(Rhynochetos jubatus)

The kagu is known as "the ghost of the forest" for its habit of skulking silently through the undergrowth. Its feathers have extra-furry edges, known as powder down, which insulate its skin and keep it dry. Often, while hunting, it stands as still as a statue, waiting for the movement of smaller animals nearby, which it strikes at with a sharp beak. Unlike other birds, the kagu also has special hairs on its beak that protect the nostrils when digging through soil for another favorite food, insects.

The kagu is renowned for its messy nests, which are often little more than a pile of leaves swept up against the trunk of a tree. Male and female take turns to sit on a single egg, which can take up to forty days to hatch. Should a ground predator approach the nest during this period, the male or female kagu pretends it has a broken wing and hops around in nearby undergrowth. This trick captures the attention of the predator and keeps it from discovering the nest.

LENGTH: 55 cm

DIET: Worms, snails, lizards, spiders, insects, and centipedes

FOUND IN: Forests and shrublands of New Caledonia

SUNBITTERN
(Eurypyga helias)

When cornered, the sunbittern opens its wings to reveal two large "eyespots" that resemble the face of a giant bird of prey. These butterfly-like markings are incredibly rare in birds and help it to scare off predators, like crocodiles and birds of prey. When the wings are closed, dappled markings and patterns provide a camouflaged cloak of invisibility.

Like the kagu, the sunbittern walks slowly, carefully scanning the ground beneath its feet for the movement of prey, which it snaps at in milliseconds. Often the sunbittern hunts in water, striding through the shallows of streams and puddles. Some scientists think this bird can fish for prey by holding a maggot in its beak and dangling it over the water to attract the interests of small fish it wants to eat.

The sunbittern is also known for its unique range of calls, including growling, hooting, and rattling sounds that it sometimes uses to frighten predators. When particularly threatened, it can produce a hissing sound that resembles a bicycle with a tire that is losing air.

LENGTH: 45 cm

DIET: Insects, crabs, spiders, shrimps, and earthworms

FOUND IN: Forests in South America from Guatemala to Brazil

TROGONS AND QUETZALS

These closely related birds live in Africa, Asia, and the Americas. They feed on insects and fruits, and rarely come down from the treetops. Fossils suggest they have been around for almost fifty million years, making them one of the oldest bird groups of all. Just under fifty species have been discovered (so far!).

BLUE-CROWNED TROGON
(Trogon curucui)

Though it has strong muscles for flight, the blue-crowned trogon rarely takes to the sky, preferring to spend most of its time shuffling between branches searching for insect prey. Much of its diet consists of hairy caterpillars, the most poisonous of which it quickly learns to avoid.

To stop itself being spotted by predators, the blue-crowned trogon turns its back to hide its colorful underparts. Like an owl, it can swivel its head around to keep its eyes on predators as they move past. Trogons are often eaten by hawks and wild cats.

LENGTH: 24 cm

DIET: Insects, mostly caterpillars

FOUND IN: Forests and woodlands, especially in central South America

GOLDEN-HEADED QUETZAL
(Pharomachrus auriceps)

In the breeding season, the male golden-headed quetzal lets out a haunting cry that is mixed, every now and then, with a call that sounds like a horse whinnying. This strange call attracts the attention of local females and signals the beginning of the nesting season.

Pairs of golden-headed quetzals take great care finding a suitable dead tree to build a nest within. The tree needs to be soft enough to carve a hole in with the beak, but not so crumbly and rotten that the nest will fall out. For this reason, breeding pairs investigate many trees in their forest home before making their choice.

LENGTH: 33–36 cm

DIET: Fruits and insects

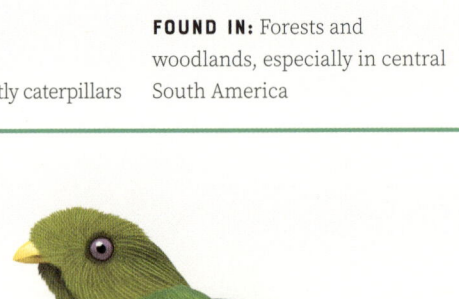

FOUND IN: Forests of Central and South America

TROPICBIRDS

In flight, tropicbirds are fast and dynamic predators of flying fish and squid. Like gannets, tropicbirds hover over their prey and then dive downward with their beak stretched out like a spear, snatching their quarry from the ocean. Three species are known, mostly from warm, tropical oceans.

RED-BILLED TROPICBIRD
(Phaethon aethereus)

Like all tropicbirds, the legs of the red-billed tropicbird are so far back on the body that walking on land has become almost impossible. Instead of walking confidently, like other birds, tropicbirds slide uncomfortably on their bellies, pushed forward by the legs.

During the breeding season, the skies above tropicbird colonies become very busy. Males and females glide and circle together with their wingtips touching. Slowly, for 300 meters or more, they drift down to the ocean surface before rising upward again. Sometimes, groups of males fly in large circles too, swinging their long tail feathers from side to side to display to watching females.

The simple nest of the red-billed tropicbird consists of a shallow pit scraped into the ground on craggy, ocean cliffs. Tropicbird chicks hatch completely naked and, for the first few days, rely totally on their parents for warmth. It takes 100 days of feeding for their chicks to grow strong enough to survive on their own.

LENGTH: 90–107 cm

DIET: Mostly fish and squid

FOUND IN: Tropical parts of the Atlantic, eastern Pacific, and Indian oceans

CUCKOOS

Cuckoos are best known for laying their eggs in the nests of other birds. This tactic, known as brood parasitism, means that adults do not need to spend their energy raising chicks. Not all cuckoo species are brood parasites. Some, like the roadrunner, raise their own chicks.

COMMON CUCKOO
(Cuculus canorus)

The feather patterns of the common cuckoo make it look like a sparrowhawk. This means that, when the cuckoo inspects the nests of other birds while looking for a place to lay its egg, the parent birds (known as hosts) keep well away.

The common cuckoo egg is also disguised. Its eggs are usually the same color and have the same speckled patterns as the eggs laid by the host. In the nest, this makes spotting them very difficult.

LENGTH: 32–34 cm

DIET: Insects, especially hairy caterpillars

FOUND IN: Open grasslands and shrublands in Africa in winter and Europe and Asia in summer

GREATER ROADRUNNER
(Geococcyx californianus)

This fearless hunter regularly eats venomous rattlesnakes, tarantulas, and giant wasps. To find its prey, the roadrunner runs at speeds of 20 miles per hour, only occasionally taking to the air. Like other cuckoos, the greater roadrunner has an extra backward-pointing toe on each foot, meaning that it leaves X-shaped footprints in the sand.

To survive cold nights in the desert, the roadrunner drops its body temperature and goes into a hibernation-like sleep. In the morning, to wake its brain up, the roadrunner basks in the sun.

LENGTH: 52–54 cm

DIET: Reptiles, mice, insects, and spiders

FOUND IN: Deserts and scrublands of southwestern USA and northern Mexico

CUCKOO-ROLLERS

Cuckoo-rollers look like cuckoos, but they come from a different bird group known as the Leptosomidae. Once, millions of years ago, there may have been many different types of this charismatic bird. Today, only one species remains.

CUCKOO-ROLLER
(Leptosomus discolor)

Still as a statue, the cuckoo-roller spends most of its day standing on a treetop perch, scanning its rainforest surroundings. When prey, such as a skittering lizard or a chameleon, accidentally makes a sound, its large head, complete with binocular-vision eyes, swings around. Next, the cuckoo-roller dashes from its perch to make the kill before bringing its meal back to the perch for eating. This hunting technique, known as a sally, is also used by hawks and other birds of prey.

Communities in Madagascar know the strange, secretive cuckoo-roller very well, because it features in myths and legends. When the cuckoo-roller performs its mating displays, which involve flying skyward toward the sun before plummeting toward the ground, local people believe that the weather will be hot and sunny later in the day.

LENGTH: 38–50 cm

DIET: Chameleons, lizards, and large insects, including stick insects and grasshoppers

FOUND IN: Forests and woodlands across Madagascar and the Comoro Islands

MOUSEBIRDS

With soft, fuzzy feathers and a habit of scurrying through leaves in search of fruits and berries, the mousebirds live up to their name. This small group of birds can dangle off branches using their strong claws. Their grip is supported by thumb-like toes that can be flexed backward or forward.

WHITE-BACKED MOUSEBIRD
(Colius colius)

When roosting together at night, white-backed mousebirds can be confused with bats. They engage in mutual preening, taking time to carefully comb one another's feathers to keep them healthy. In the morning, the white-backed mousebird basks in the sun. This blast of heat energy helps it digest its food more quickly.

In a single day, the white-backed mousebird can feed upon up to thirty different kinds of fruit. Occasionally, this species also strips leaf buds from fruit trees, upsetting farmers. It is probably for this reason that the white-backed mousebird is very wary of humans.

LENGTH: 29–32 cm, including tail feathers

FOUND IN: Scrublands of southern Africa

DIET: Fruits, leaf buds, nectar, and seeds

BLUE-NAPED MOUSEBIRD
(Urocolius macrourus)

In groups of up to fifty, the blue-naped mousebird flies laps around its dry woodland habitat, stopping every hundred meters or so to feed on fruiting trees. As long as the trees continue to produce fruit, these neighborhood circuits are memorized and repeated every day.

Like other mousebirds, the toes of the blue-naped mousebird are multi-purpose. With all four toes facing forward, it can acrobatically scurry along branches; with two toes facing backward and two facing forward, it can grip fruit like a monkey.

LENGTH: 33–36 cm, including tail feathers

FOUND IN: Semi-deserts and dry woodlands across Africa

DIET: Fruits, leaves, flowers, and leaf buds

TURACOS AND GO-AWAY-BIRDS

With their large crests and colorful green and red feather patterns, turacos are eye-catching birds that live in forests, woodlands, and savannas throughout Africa. Unusually, young turacos have claws on the wings that they use for climbing branches and twigs.

GUINEA TURACO
(Tauraco persa)

When the breeding season begins, the guinea turaco lets out an ear-piercing song that consists of up to sixteen notes, each a fraction of a second long. Its green plumage is made using a special protein in the feathers called turacoverdin, which is not found in any other group of birds.

Like all turacos, the fourth toe of the guinea turaco can face forward or be pulled backward to the rear of the foot. This means it can be used for grasping branches while climbing through the forest canopy looking for fruit.

LENGTH: 40–43 cm

DIET: Fruits

FOUND IN: Forests throughout western and central Africa

GRAY GO-AWAY-BIRD
(Crinifer concolor)

The so-called "go-away-birds" get their name from their strange alarm calls. This unusual call, delivered as a long and drawn out "KWEH" noise, sounds from a distance like someone saying "GO AWAY!" The ear-piercing call is said to be so effective that other birds and mammals either freeze or flee when they hear it.

When hunting for fruit, the gray go-away-bird joins "feeding parties" of up to thirty individuals. Moving around in large groups means that there are more eyes on the lookout for both food and predators.

LENGTH: 47–50 cm

DIET: Fruits, flowers, buds, leaves, and insects

FOUND IN: Woodlands across central and southern Africa

GET TO KNOW BIRDS NEAR YOU

Because of changes to our planet caused by humans, there are a lot fewer birds than there used to be. Today, about half of all bird species are going down in number each year. Birds clearly need friends, so here's what you can do to help...

DON'T FORGET TO LOOK UP!

Looking to find a connection with birds? Look up! Many people forget that birds live among us, busying their lives with finding food, nesting, or fighting for territory. A simple upward glance every now and then can work wonders for helping you understand your local birds that bit better.

TUNE INTO YOUR NEIGHBORHOOD BIRDS

Another trick to learning about local birds is to tune into nature's finest playlist—birdsong! Birds sing mostly in the early hours, but many species call during the day, particularly if there are predators around. Many apps or websites exist to help you identify any calls you hear regularly.

FEEDING TIME

Filled with nuts or seeds, birdfeeders can give local birds an extra snack to keep them going during periods when their own food becomes hard to find. Just remember to clean your feeders regularly to stop germs from gathering there.

NEST-BOXES

Adding nest-boxes to houses or schools means there are more nesting places for nearby birds to use. Some nest-boxes can be built from scratch; others can be purchased pre-made and ready to hang. By adjusting the size of the entrance hole, you can influence the kinds of birds that might nest there.

CITIZEN SCIENCE

To find out more about how habitats are changing because of humans, scientists ask local people, including schoolchildren, to count birds on their behalf. By gathering lots of data about bird sightings, scientists can look at how bird numbers change year on year.

JOIN A BIRD GROUP

Across the world, in towns and cities, there are people like you with an interest in birds. These groups might be associated with national bird charities or they might be connected to local nature reserves. Often, these groups are very involved in bird conservation, meaning you can do your bit to protect local nature by getting involved with them.

INDEX

A

ALBATROSS	146, 166
BLACK-BROWED	146
WANDERING	146
ANTBIRD, OCELLATED	136
ANTSHRIKE, BARRED	136
ANT-TANAGER, RED-CROWNED	91
APOSTLEBIRD	59
AUK	144, 145, 174
RAZOR-BILLED	144

B

BABBLER	76, 77
ABBOTT'S	77
ARROW-MARKED	83
FALCATED WREN	77
JUNGLE	82
PUFF-THROATED	76
BANANAQUIT	114
BEE-EATER	142, 143
EUROPEAN	143
BELLBIRD, NEW ZEALAND	79
BELLBIRD, WHITE	67
BIRD OF PARADISE	57, 60, 61, 62, 140
KING	60
RAGGIANA	60
WILSON'S	61
BITTERN	164, 165
GREAT	165
BLACKBIRD	34, 90
BLACKBIRD, EURASIAN	116
BLACKEYE, MOUNTAIN	126
BLUEBIRD, WESTERN	117
BLUETHROAT	94
BLUE TIT, EURASIAN	118
BOBOLINK	90
BOOBY	156, 157
BLUE-FOOTED	157
MASKED	157
BOWERBIRD, SATIN	63
BOWERBIRD, VOGELKOP	63
BRUSHTURKEY, AUSTRALIAN	40
BUDGERIGAR	50, 51
BULBUL, LIGHT-VENTED	56
BULBUL, RED-WHISKERED	56
BULLFINCH, EURASIAN	72
BUNTING, PAINTED	91
BUSHTIT, LONG-TAILED	86
BUSTARD, BENGAL FLORICAN	33
BUSTARD, GREAT	33
BUTCHERBIRD	106, 130, 131
GRAY	131

C

CARACARA	18
BLACK	19
CARDINAL	91
CASSOWARY	28, 29, 30
SOUTHERN	29
CHACHALACA	40, 41, 42
RUFOUS-VENTED	41
CHICKADEE, GRAY-HEADED	119
CHIFFCHAFF, COMMON	41, 85
CHOUGH, WHITE-WINGED	59
CISTICOLA, GOLDEN-HEADED	64
CISTICOLA, ZITTING	64
COCKATIEL	49
COCKATOO, PALM	48
COCKATOO, SULFUR-CRESTED	49
COCK-OF-THE-ROCK, ANDEAN	66
CONDOR, ANDEAN	24
CONDOR, CALIFORNIA	25
CORMORANT	148, 149
DOUBLE-CRESTED	148
LITTLE PIED	149
RED-LEGGED	148
COTINGA	66, 67
POMPADOUR	66
CRANE	150, 151, 170
DEMOISELLE	151
GRAY CROWNED	150
RED-CROWNED	150
SARUS	151
CROW	68, 103, 131, 139, 174
NEW CALEDONIAN	68
CUCKOO	39, 41, 96, 116, 180
COMMON	180
CUCKOO-ROLLER	181
CUCKOO-WEAVER	129
CURASSOW	40, 41, 42
NOCTURNAL	41
CURRAWONG	130, 131
BLACK	131
CUTIA, HIMALAYAN	83

D

DOVE	138, 139
ROCK	139
DUCK	152, 153, 158, 159, 166
MANDARIN	153

E

EAGLE	16, 17, 20, 22, 25, 47, 48, 100, 154, 162
BALD	16
PHILIPPINE	16
STELLER'S SEA	17
EIDER, COMMON	152
EMU	28, 30, 31

F

FAIRYWREN, SUPERB	70
FAIRYWREN, WALLACE'S	70
FALCON	18, 130
PEREGRINE	18, 48, 50, 139
PYGMY	19, 125

FERNBIRD, NEW ZEALAND		75
FINCH		72, 73, 122
FINFOOT		170, 171
AFRICAN		171
FIREFINCH, RED-BILLED		72, 129
FIRETAIL, BEAUTIFUL		122
FLAMINGO		154, 155
AMERICAN		155
CHILEAN		155
GREATER		54
LESSER		154
FLICKER, NORTHERN		36
FLYCATCHER		34, 94, 95, 120, 121
BROWN-CRESTED		120
EUROPEAN PIED		95
INDIAN PARADISE		134
MALAGASY PARADISE		134
VERMILION		120
YELLOWISH		121
FRIGATEBIRD		148, 149
MAGNIFICENT		149
FROGMOUTH		10, 11
TAWNY		11
FRUIT-HUNTER		117
FULVETTA, RUFOUS-WINGED		76

G

GALAH	48
GANNET	156, 179
NORTHERN	156
GO-AWAY-BIRD, GRAY	181
GOLDFINCH, AMERICAN	73
GOOSE, BAR-HEADED	158
GOOSE, CANADA	158
GRASSBIRD, BRISTLED	74
GRASSWREN	70, 71
DUSKY	71
STRIATED	71
GREBE, AUSTRALASIAN	160
GREBE, GREAT CRESTED	160
GROUND FINCH, VAMPIRE	115
GUINEAFOWL	42, 43
VULTURINE	43
GULL	149, 162, 174
GREAT BLACK-BACKED	162
GREBE, AUSTRALASIAN	160

H

HAWK	16, 20, 21, 22, 26, 35, 134, 160, 178
AFRICAN HARRIER	20
EURASIAN GOSHAWK	21
GALÁPAGOS	21
HAWAIIAN	20
HERON	164, 172
BLACK	164
HONEYEATER	51, 78, 79
MACGREGOR'S	79
NEW HOLLAND	78
HONEYGUIDE	36, 37, 39
GREATER	37
HOOPOE	38, 39
EURASIAN	39
HORNBILL, KNOBBED	38
HORNBILL, NORTHERN GROUND	38
HORNERO, WING-BANDED	99
HUMMINGBIRD	14, 15, 78, 110, 114, 120
BEE	14
GIANT	15
RUBY-THROATED	15

I

IBIS	34, 164, 172
AFRICAN SACRED	164
'I'IWI	73
INDIGOBIRD, DUSKY	72, 129

J

JABIRU	172
JAY	68, 69
CALIFORNIA SCRUB	69

K

KAGU	176
KĀKĀ	52
KĀKĀPŌ	53
KEA	52
KINGFISHER	127, 140, 141, 142
BLACK-BACKED DWARF	141
BROWN-HEADED PARADISE	140
COMMON	140
KITE	16, 20, 22, 23, 26, 50, 134
BLACK	22
MISSISSIPPI	23
RED	22
SNAIL	23
KIWI, NORTH ISLAND BROWN	28, 30
KOOKABURRA, LAUGHING	141

L

LAPWING, SOCIABLE	81, 174
LARK	80, 81
GREATER HOOPOE	80
RUFOUS-NAPED	81
SAND	81
LAUGHINGTHRUSH, WHITE-CRESTED	82
LEAF WARBLER	84, 85
LIMESTONE	84
PALLAS'S	84
LIMPKIN	170, 171
LONGTAIL, CRICKET	65
LOON	160, 161
ARCTIC	161
COMMON	161
LORIKEET, RAINBOW	50
LORIKEET, SCALY-BREASTED	50
LYREBIRD, ALBERT'S	87

LYREBIRD, SUPERB	87
GANNET	156, 179
NORTHERN	156
GO-AWAY-BIRD, GRAY	181
GOLDFINCH, AMERICAN	73
GOOSE, BAR-HEADED	158
GOOSE, CANADA	158
GRASSBIRD, BRISTLED	74
GRASSWREN	70, 71
DUSKY	71
STRIATED	71
GREBE, AUSTRALASIAN	160
GREBE, GREAT CRESTED	160
GROUND FINCH, VAMPIRE	115
GUINEAFOWL	42, 43
VULTURINE	43
GULL	149, 162, 174
GREAT BLACK-BACKED	162
GREBE, AUSTRALASIAN	160

M

MACAW	34, 54
HYACINTH	54
SCARLET	54
MADANGA	101
MALEO	40
MALLARD	152
MANAKIN	88, 89, 122
ARARIPE	88
LONG-TAILED	89
STRIOLATED	89
MARTIN	112, 113
WHITE-EYED RIVER	113
MEADOWLARK, WESTERN	90
MINER, SLENDER-BILLED	98
MOORHEN, DUSKY	170
MOTMOT	142, 143
TRINIDAD	143
MOUSEBIRD	182
BLUE-NAPED	182
WHITE-BACKED	182
MURRE, THICK-BILLED	144
MURRELET, JAPANESE	145
MYNA, COMMON	109

N

NIGHTJAR, EURASIAN	10
NUTCRACKER, EURASIAN	69

O

OILBIRD	10, 11
OSPREY	16, 17
OSTRICH	28, 30, 31
COMMON	30
OVENBIRD	93, 98, 99
OWL	35, 44, 45, 46, 47, 178
BUFFY FISH	47
BURROWING	47
COMMON BARN	44
GREAT GRAY	46
ORIENTAL BAY	45
RED	44
SNOWY	46
SOOTY	45
OXPECKER	137
RED-BILLED	137
YELLOW-BILLED	137

P

PARAKEET	54, 55
MONK	55
PAURAQUE, COMMON	10
PARROT	41, 48, 49, 50, 51, 52, 53, 54, 55, 109
GRAY	55
SCARLET-CHEEKED FIG	51
PEAFOWL, INDIAN	42
PELICAN	164, 166, 167
AUSTRALIAN	166
DALMATIAN	166
PERUVIAN	167
PENGUIN	46, 168, 169
EMPEROR	168
KING	168
LITTLE	169
ROYAL	169
PETREL	146, 147
SOUTHERN GIANT	147, 169
WILSON'S STORM	147
PIGEON	51, 138, 139, 166
COMMON WOOD	139
THICK-BILLED GREEN	138
VICTORIAN CROWNED	138
PIPIT, PADDYFIELD	100
PIPIT, WATER	101
PITTA, FAIRY	103
PITTA, MALAYAN BANDED	102
PITTA, NOISY	103
PITTA, WESTERN HOODED	102
POCHARD, MADAGASCAR	153
PUFFIN, ATLANTIC	145

Q

QUELEA, RED-BILLED	124
QUETZAL, GOLDEN-HEADED	178

R

RAIL, GUAM	170
RAVEN, COMMON	68
RHEA	30, 31
GREATER	31
RIFLEBIRD, MAGNIFICENT	62
ROADRUNNER, GREATER	180
ROBIN	58, 132
SCARLET	58
WHITE-BREASTED	58
ROBIN, EUROPEAN	94
ROLLER, LILAC-BREASTED	142
RUFF	175
RUSH TYRANT, MANY-COLORED	121

S

SANDGROUSE, PIN-TAILED	32
SANDGROUSE, TIBETAN	32
SANDPIPER, WESTERN	174
SAPSUCKER	36, 37
RED-BREASTED	37
SATINBIRD, CRESTED	57
SATINBIRD, YELLOW-BREASTED	57
SAW-WING	112, 113
FANTI	113
SCIMITAR BABBLER, INDIAN	135
SCIMITAR BABBLER, SRI LANKA	135
SCYTHEBILL, BROWN-BILLED	98
SHOEBILL	164, 165, 166
SHRIKE	106, 107, 128, 131
GREAT GRAY	106
LOGGERHEAD	107
RED-BACKED	107
SICKLEBILL, BLACK	61
SILVEREYE	126
SKIMMER, BLACK	162
SKYLARK, EURASIAN	80
SPARROW	81, 93, 96, 97, 117
CAPE	96
CHESTNUT	97
HOUSE	96
RUSSET	97
SONG	92
WHITE-CROWNED	92
SPIDERHUNTER, SPECTACLED	111
SPINEBILL, EASTERN	78
SPOONBILL	164, 165
ROSEATE	165
STARLING	51, 108, 109, 117, 127
CAPE	108
COMMON	108
HILDEBRANDT'S	109
STONE-CURLEW, BUSH	175
STORK, MARABOU	173
STORK, WHITE	172
STORK, WHITE-BELLIED	173
SUNBIRD	110, 111, 114
BLACK-BELLIED	111
MALACHITE	110
SAHYADRI	110
SUNBITTERN	176, 177
SWALLOW	112, 117
BARN	112
LESSER STRIPED	112
SWAN	158, 159, 166
BLACK	159
MUTE	159
SWIFT, COMMON	12
SWIFTLET, HIMALAYAN	13

T

TANAGER, SWALLOW	114
TANAGER, WHITE-CAPPED	115
TERN	162, 163
ARCTIC	163
THRUSH	76, 116, 117
GREAT	116
TINAMOU	30, 31
GREAT	31
TIT, PYGMY	86
TIT, SULTAN	118
TITMOUSE, BRIDLED	119
TOUCAN, KEEL-BILLED	35
TOUCAN, LETTERED ARACARI	35
TOUCAN, PLATE-BILLED MOUNTAIN	34
TOUCAN, TOCO	34
TREESWIFT, CRESTED	13
TROGON, BLUE-CROWNED	178
TROPICBIRD, RED-BILLED	179
TURACO, GUINEA	183
TURKEY, WILD	43

V

VULTURE (SEE ALSO CONDOR)	16, 20, 22, 23, 24, 173
BEARDED	27
KING	25
LAPPET-FACED	26
RÜPPELL'S	27
WHITE-RUMPED	26

W

WADER	174, 175
WAGTAIL, WHITE	100
WARBLER	65, 74, 75, 76, 93, 104, 105
AFRICAN YELLOW	105
AQUATIC	104
AUSTRALIAN REED	105
COMMON GRASSHOPPER	74
COMMON REED	104
GRAY-CAPPED	65
PROTHONOTARY	93
SRI LANKA BUSH	75
WAXBILL	122, 128
ORANGE-CHEEKED	122
WAXWING, BOHEMIAN	123
WEAVER, SOCIABLE	125
WEAVER, VILLAGE	124
WEAVER, WHITE-HEADED BUFFALO	125
WHEATEAR, DESERT	95
WHITE-EYE, BONIN	127
WHITE-EYE, GOLDEN	127
WOODCREEPER, OLIVACEOUS	99
WOODHOOPOE	38, 39
GREEN	39
WOODPECKER	36, 61
GREAT SPOTTED	36
WOODSWALLOW, FIJI	130
WOODSWALLOW, WHITE-BREASTED	130
WREN, COBB'S	132
WREN, EURASIAN	133
WREN, GIANT	132
WYDAH, PIN-TAILED	128

GLOSSARY

BARBULES minute notches on the edge of a feather that scatter light in different directions, creating an iridescent effect

BROOD PARASITISM a strategy that some birds use to save energy, by relying on others to take care of their chicks

CARRION the decaying flesh of dead animals, scavenged by vultures and other birds

CASQUE a bony extension on the skulls of some birds, like the knobbed hornbill, which can act as armor or an echo chamber to help their calls travel further

CRECHE a nursery where lots of chicks are looked after communally by many parent birds

CROP a chamber in the throat where birds store food and make crop milk for their young

ECHOLOCATION a method of navigation that relies on rebounding soundwaves

FLEDGE when a young bird first leaves the nest

GASTROLITHS pebbles or stones that are held in the stomach to help grind up food, sometimes also known as grit

GLEANING a technique for finding insects by running the beak through small cracks and crevices

HONEYDEW a sugary liquid, like nectar, produced by tiny, aphid-like insects

HOSTS the parent birds who look after hatchlings that have been placed in their nest by brood parasites, like cuckoos

INCUBATION the process of sitting on an egg to keep it warm until it hatches

KERATIN a protein that hardens birds' beaks, and also makes up human fingernails and rhino horns

KLEPTOPARASITISM a strategy that some birds use to save energy, by stealing food caught by other birds

LARVAE the young of insects

LEKS proving grounds where male birds of some species gather to show off against rivals, for the chance to pair with females

MIGRATION the seasonal movement of birds between breeding and wintering grounds

MOBBING the gathering together of a number of small birds to harass and drive off a larger predator

PASSERINES birds of the order Passeriformes, known as perching birds, who make up over half of all bird species

POLLINATORS birds who help plants reproduce, by carrying pollen from the male part of one plant to the female part of another

REGURGITATION the vomiting of partially digested food, either as a substance to feed chicks or as a material to help make nests

ROOSTING the gathering together of a large number of birds to rest

SCATS piles of droppings, often containing seeds that can then germinate and grow

SPICULES short spines on the feet of some birds of prey that help them grip onto slippery prey, like fish

SYRINX a voice box that enables a wide range of calls

TAXONOMY the science of organizing things into categories, like birds into species and families

THERMALS a current of warm, upward-moving air that some birds use to gain altitude and use less energy while flying

WATTLE a fleshy growth on the face or neck of some birds, like bellbirds and turkeys

Encyclopedia of Birds © 2025 Quarto Publishing plc.
Text © 2025 Jules Howard.
Illustrations © 2025 Namasri Niumim.

First Published in 2025 by Wide Eyed Editions, an imprint of The Quarto Group.
Quarto Publishing plc, 100 Cummings Center, Suite 265D, Beverly, MA 01915
USA. T +1 978-282-9590 www.Quarto.com

The right of Jules Howard to be identified as the author and Namasri Niumim to be identified as the illustrator of this work has been asserted by them in accordance with the Copyright, Designs and Patents Act, 1988 (UK).

All rights reserved.

No part of this publication may be reproduced, stored in a retrieval system, or transmitted, in any form, or by any means, electrical, mechanical, photocopying, recording or otherwise without the prior written permission of the publisher or a licence permitting restricted copying.

ISBN 978-0-7112-9528-5
EISBN 978-0-7112-9529-2

The illustrations were created digitally
Set in Bourton and Source Serif Pro

Publisher Debbie Foy
Editorial Director Lucy Brownridge
Editor Poppy David
Art Director Karissa Santos
Designer Lyli Feng and Robyn Makings
Production Controller Dawn Cameron

Manufactured in Guangdong, China TT102024

9 8 7 6 5 4 3 2 1

MIX
Paper | Supporting responsible forestry
FSC
www.fsc.org
FSC® C016973